FISH HOUSE SECRETS

FISH   HOUSE   SECRETS

Kathy Stinson

Thistledown Press Ltd.

Canadian Cataloguing in Publication Data
Stinson, Kathy, 1952—
  Fish house secrets
  ISBN 0-920633-91-9   1-895449-10-3 (PBK)
I. Title.
PS8587.T56FS 1992   C813'.54   C92-098036-8
PR9199.3.S75F5 1992

Book design by A.M. Forrie
Cover painting by Iris Hauser
Typeset by Thistledown Press Ltd.
Printed and bound in Canada by
Hignell Printing., Winnipeg

Thistledown Press Ltd.
668 East Place
Saskatoon, Saskatchewan
S7J 2Z5

Acknowledgements:
Quotation from "Dreams" by Langston Hughes,
The Dream-Keeper, © 1932, Alfred A. Knopf
Quotation from *Where the Wild Things Are* by
Maurice Sendak, © 1963, Harper and Row

This book has been published with the assistance of
The Canada Council and the Saskatchewan Arts Board

Dedicated with thanks
to Peter
for taking me there

Hold fast to dreams
For if dreams die
Life is a broken-winged bird
That cannot fly

— Langston Hughes

Friday

Chad

I don't know where to start. Should I tell you about Jill coming to the Fish House that first time? Or should I tell you about the accident? Or about what I saw on the beach before the night of the storm?

The beginning. That's what Billy J. always says. He was my English teacher last year in Grade Ten. Why not start at the beginning?

I was born in Toronto. My parents are — were — Emily Merrill, painter — maybe you've heard of her, and Gordon Merrill, professor of mathematics. Please note that I did not say my father is a math prof, or a professor of math. He is a "professor of mathematics". My father is very particular about that.

Somehow I don't think this is the beginning that Billy J. was talking about. Even though my father *is* a very particular kind of guy. Worse since the accident.

There it is again. The accident last fall. Maybe that's the beginning. Except for my mom. For her it was the end.

It was slippery. It started to rain when we were cheering for the winning touchdown. Mom was on her way to pick me and a couple of other guys up after the game. This truck skidded on a curve. You know how the roads get slick when it first starts to rain? Well, this truck coming toward her just slid right over on the curve and creamed her through the guardrail into a ditch.

Usually me and my friends took the bus home from games, but it would have taken about three transfers to get back from this game because of where it was, and it didn't start till late, so my mom said she'd pick us up. I guess I don't need to tell you I wish we'd taken the bus. It's probably not very cool to say so, but I miss her. A lot.

But what's almost worse is how my dad has been since then. It's like all of a sudden he thinks he's got to be two parents. And it's not like we were exactly pals before. We didn't hate each other or anything. Don't get me wrong. We've just never had all that much to do with each other, that's all. We might talk about the Blue Jays and spring training and who was getting traded, stuff like that. We've been to the odd game too. And he gives me fifty bucks every term I keep up a B+ average, as long as "mathematics" isn't one of the subjects that slips below a B. He's a nice guy. We've just never been what you'd call close.

But when my mom died, he got different. Like fathers on TV. You know, wanting to do things with their kids all the time, talking serious with them. And it's like he wants to take care of me. I'm fifteen years old. I don't need to be taken care of. I guess he thinks he's making up for me not having a mother any more, I don't know. All I know is after three days cooped up in the car and two nights in motels getting to Gran and Gramp's summer place where the rugged hills overlook the sea, he's really bugging me.

And I'm not prepared for how being there again brings her back.

Jill

God, am I stupid. There's no way I can get to Sheila's before it gets dark. Not now.

I should've known something was wrong when I passed that tired-looking old house with the rusted old shell of a car out front, and the cracked pot of weeds and geraniums beside the steps. Why didn't I turn back then?

It's that lady in the store's fault. She told me the Merritts' place was down this road. That's why I kept going. Okay, maybe I should've got better directions from Sheila, but I didn't know then I was definitely coming. And I left in kind of a hurry.

Besides, I wasn't dead sure it was the wrong road till it kind of petered out to this grassy track.By thehese gulls were circling around and the sea was calling to me. I had to come down here. Just for a few minutes.

The ground to the right of the path falls away to a tumble of rocks. The waves are washing the shore, it's almost hypnotic, and I stay longer than I mean to, poking along, collecting shells and a few stones. It's heaven to be down by the sea again. Like a dream.

The lonesome squawk of a gull snaps me out of it. It raises its wings, and soon it's only a speck. It reminds me how far I have to go, back to the highway to try the other road, the one we passed just before this one, me and the guy I hitched a ride with out of Halifax this morning. At least I guess that's the road I was supposed to take.

But there's no way I can get back to the highway before dark, never mind find Sheila's cottage. What am I going to do? Curl up for the night under one of the old fish boxes that the sea's tossed up on the rocks? Or under the bushes back by the path? No, wait.

Out at the end of the point where that seagull disappeared there's a house. At the edge of the rock beach. From here it looks like there's no glass in its windows. It must be empty.

I climb back to the path. I'm sure the house is empty. I can stay there for the night and try for Sheila's again in the morning.

Chad

Dad gives three short toots of the horn as usual — it's never two, never four — as the car lurches over the familiar bumps of rock in the driveway. I hardly wait till the car stops before I've got the door open. I couldn't stand to watch him meticulously entering the mileage and our time of arrival in the travel diary he keeps in the tidy glove box.

Besides, I want to feel the sun on my face and the sea air whipping against me. And the sea is out there, as blue today as the upper storey triangle of the white frame house that looks over it.

Gramp hasn't cut the Queen Anne's lace this year that grows all over the lawn. The bobbing heads go snickety against my legs when I run out to the hill in front of the house. Yeah, *snickety*. One of the things I love about Dutchman's Bay is how much sharper everything seems here, the colours, the sounds, everything just feels — I don't know — sharper. I can't wait to get down where I can feel the spray blowing in off the sea and smell the seaweed washed up in last week's storm.

Dutchman's Bay — I've come here every summer since I was born. It's kind of like my grandparents' cottage, only it's not a cottage, it's an old farmhouse on the south shore of Nova Scotia.

Mom got the inspiration for a lot of her painting here. Before she met my dad she painted mostly cityscapes and once in a while the country around Toronto, old barns, stuff like that. She was good, but she'd never been to the ocean before, and Dutchman's Bay brought out something that made her work after that different, really unique. Not just the gorgeous seascapes she painted while she was here. All her work.

Gran and Gramp live most of the year in Ottawa and my parents live in Toronto (well, me and my dad now), so we don't see each other that much, except for summers. Gramp had a heart attack this winter, but just a mild one the doctor said, so I'm not ready for how different he looks when he comes out of the house. He moves so slow, kind of stiff. I guess lots of seventy-six-year-old guys move like that, but right up till last summer Gramp was walking the full length of the beach every day. It looks like this year he'll be lucky if he can even get down to the beach.

His grip on my shoulder is as strong as ever though. "Good to see you, Chad," he says.

"You too, Gramp," I say. The breeze is lifting the white wisps of his hair. He's tall, but shorter it seems than the last time I saw him, at Mom's funeral. "I'm almost as tall as you now."

"Whuh?"

I feel like I'm shouting when I say it again, "I'm almost as tall as you now." It's funny. I've always been a bit, not afraid of my grandfather exactly, but sort of. Maybe because whenever I forget to speak up and he says, "whuh?" it seems like he's mad. Which is dumb, because really he just didn't hear. And also, he's supposedly pretty proud of his only grandson. That's what Mom said anyway.

"Yes, you're getting to be a handsome young man, Chad," Gramp says. There's a sparkle in his eye. "Lot of girls in Toronto mooning over your departure this summer?" He's as big a tease as ever. His heart attack hasn't slowed him down any that way.

"Where's Gran?"

"Whuh?"

"Where's Gran?"

"Oh. She's off in the woods looking for mush-rooms."

My dad comes out to the hill. "Hello, Father," he says.

"I'm glad you're here, Gordon," Gramp says. "Let's get your car unpacked and settle you in."

"You go sit down," Dad says. "Chad and I will bring our things in. Come on, Chad."

Gramp says, "I'll give you a hand."

"The doctor said you're to take it easy."

Gramp grumbles something and follows us to the car. It looks like he isn't planning on doing much "taking it easy" this summer.

Jill

Scrubby bushes scratch at my legs as I run toward the empty house. There's traces of weathered paint round the window and door frames, bleached so the whole house is almost the same grey. A long sunporch faces out to sea. This might be better than going to Sheila's. There'll be no one here to ask any questions.

The side door, toward the back of the house, is hanging on one hinge. I go inside. Strips of lath and plaster hang from the walls like ripped out guts, glass and plaster crunch underfoot. Burn marks scar the walls, and beer bottles and hamburger cartons litter the floor. Someone's left scraps of food too, not very long ago. A chill breeze blows in a clinging damp. I stumble back outside. Above, a seagull shrieks.

I'm not waiting around for whoever was here before. I run. I run till the grassy track widens to road again. Then, slowing down till I'm just hobbling, I clutch at the stitch in my side.

Oh, Mark, what am I doing here? Why didn't I talk to you before I left? You're not just a brother, you're my best friend. Not to mention my *only* friend except Jeff and Charlotte. You might've talked me out of it. Or maybe you would've come with me, would you? Probably not. Amy really needs you to help her through everything, doesn't she? I'll be back in a couple of days. But you don't know that, do you? I better phone you in the morning, so you don't worry. Except Ma'll tell you I've just gone to Sheila's, won't she? If you see each other. Between her shift at the restaurant, whichever one she's at today, and yours at the Irving gas, you might not. And you'll probably be avoiding her anyway. I know you've heard enough about how the baby is Amy's problem and you have to finish school. It's not fair how Ma's on your case all the time, is it, after she's screwed up her own life so bad. I think you and Amy getting married is a good idea. I might even move in with you. That'd be a nice family, wouldn't it? A mom and dad, a baby and an aunt. Better than what we've got now.

The sun's down into the tops of the trees. I've gotta figure out what I'm doing tonight, never mind in the morning. A big black bird's watching me from the top of a tree, like a judge. *So I made a mistake. I'll find somewhere to sleep. Don't hassle me.*

Merrill — the name on one of the mailboxes by the side of the road. Why didn't I see that on the way in? It's why that stupid woman in the store sent me down here. She confused Merritt with Merrill. What an idiot.

It's another couple of hours back to the highway. Maybe the Merrills are away and the house is unlocked. Or maybe they don't lock their car.

I follow the long driveway. There's a sign on a gate, Trespassers Will Be Prosecuted. But I just need a spot to curl up for the night. I'll be gone before they're up to start prosecuting trespassers in the morning. I climb the gate.

Chad

There's not a whole lot left of the afternoon. Gran has come back from her mushroom-picking and is having "a little lie-down" as she calls it before starting supper. Dad wants Gramp to have a rest too while we go for a walk on the beach. I'm dying to go to the beach, but I'd rather go by myself. Gramp insists he's not tired, he's been looking forward to a game of chess, out on the hill in front of the house. I agree to play, thinking Dad will go on to the beach without me. But he doesn't.

We don't need him to, but he sets up the portable table for us. Gramp and I bring the two chairs that are always on the hill around to either side. For a minute I think Dad's going to get one for himself, so he can watch us play, but he comes back instead with a cloth to wipe the dust off the table. He stands there while Gramp and I set up our pieces. Gramp's black. I'm white.

"I thought you were going to the beach," I say, hoping it's not too obvious that I wish he would.

"That's okay," he says, "I can wait until your game is over."

I guess I wasn't too obvious.

It would be bad enough if he just wanted to watch, but of course that's not all he does. After a couple of suggestions he makes about my strategy, I say, "Do you want to play, Dad? I don't mind, really. I'll go to the beach or something if you do."

"No. That's okay. You play."

"Bring me my field-glasses, Gordon, would you?" Gramp says. "They should be on the windowsill in the kitchen."

Gramp's a pretty keen birdwatcher, so he doesn't like to be outside without his binoculars for very long.

Dad brings them out. They're good ones. Mom bought them for Gramp a couple of years ago after a really successful show in Calgary. Dad leaves us to our chess game kind of suddenly then, going off behind me somewhere, maybe to the woods, or down to the rocks, or the Fish House. It doesn't really matter. At least he's gone.

"It's your turn, Chad," Gramp says. He looks through his binoculars at a swallow which has swooped out the top window of the barn and sailed over the bay bushes and Queen Anne's lace, and landed finally on a hydro wire.

I move my white knight out of the black rook's path.

Gramp studies the board briefly, running a large hand over his leathery face. He slides a bishop forward to capture my knight.

How dumb can I get? "Guess I was thinking about something else," I offer lamely. I half hope Gramp might acknowledge what a pest Dad's been.

As if he knows what I'm thinking, Gramp says, "Your father hasn't had an easy time of it this year. This summer will be very difficult for him."

Okay, so I'm a heel. But it's not exactly going to be easy for me either. Doesn't anybody know I miss her too? So I didn't cry at her funeral. It doesn't mean I don't care she's not here. I shove a pawn forward.

Below the hill and off in the distance the surf is rolling in. Mom and I planted ourselves in the dunes behind the beach last summer, just beyond Tickle Creek, and did some painting of the rocks along the shore, of the dune grass casting shadows and drawing circles in the sand, of the sky. So many shades of grey to play with in the clouds and the endless sea.

Someone is walking on the beach this afternoon, just a speck. I might not have noticed if it weren't for the red T-shirt. Then there's Zooks too, bounding out of the waves. Zooks is the neighbour's black Lab, so it's probably Ian down at the water's edge.

Mom loved Zooks. She was there when he was born four summers ago. Gees, it's funny what hits out the blue, and reminds me of her.

It's my turn again and I move my white queen into position to attack one of Gramp's knights, checking first this time that I'm not putting my queen in jeopardy. While Gramp studies the board I pick up my captured knight and rub my thumb over the horse's smooth back. "This is a cool chess set, isn't it, Gramp." I remember to speak up so he can hear me. "I've never seen one like this before."

"Belongs to a friend of mine. Hand-sculpted by his great-grandfather and handed down through the generations."

"So how come you've got it?"

"Jack left it with me thirteen years ago, temporarily, when he got himself into a bit of trouble. With the law, you could say. He figured he'd be on the move for a while."

"Wow. What'd he do that was so awful?"

"Depends who's doing the telling." Gramp wraps his fist around one of the carved chunks of stone. "He stayed here for a time. We were playing when he told me he had to leave. Said when things cooled off, he'd come back for it."

"Where'd he go?"

Gramp shrugs. "Wouldn't tell me. If anybody came looking for him, it would be better, he said, if I didn't know anything."

"But he never came back?"

"Not yet." Gramp stares up past the house toward the Old Barn.

I set the knight down beside the board. I don't feel like finishing the game.

Gramp says, "But you know, Jack had courage in his own way, young and headstrong. I can almost imagine him striding in over the hills, and finding us playing here."

I shake my head, swallow. "It's your turn."

Just as we're finishing up, Dad comes back from wherever. "How about that beach walk, Chad?" he suggests.

"It's getting kind of close to supper, isn't it?"

"I'll go ask Gran."

Knowing her, she'll make sure there's time for a walk. No one goes out of their way more than Gran trying to keep everybody in the family happy.

The door snaps shut behind him. Maybe it's my imagination, but the look I catch from Gramp seems to say, "Have a heart, take a walk with your father."

Dad comes back out with a sweater for him and a sweatshirt for me. "There's time to go as far as Whaleback, Gran says. She'll hold dinner."

"I don't need a sweatshirt, Dad. It's warm."

"The sun's getting low, son," he says, pulling on his sweater. "It won't feel warm for much longer."

I sigh and tie my sweatshirt around my waist. We head down the hill and across our neighbour's pasture. Their bull looks up as we pass. "Hello, George," Dad says, and George goes back to munching his grass. Up by the yellow house a few turkeys are strutting around. When we reach the edge of the woods Dad waits for me to catch up.

A wide path meanders over roots and mossy rocks. There are rustlings of birds and small animals deeper in the undergrowth.

"You used to think there were monkeys in these woods," Dad says. "Do you remember that?"

I want to say, "Sure, I used to stop and look in every hole to see if there was anything in it too. So what." But I know I'm being a jerk, so I sort of laugh and say, "Yeah." What else can I say?

We're out of the woods and crossing the meadow when Zooks comes charging through the long grass. Ian's not far behind.

Gramp isn't the only one who's changed since I last saw him. Ian is only four months older than me, but this summer he looks way older. Not just because he's taller. His red T-shirt is hanging from where he's knotted it through a pant-loop so it's obvious how much broader his chest and shoulders are too. There's something else I can't pin down – the way he sort of swaggers?

"Good to see you, old buddy." Ian punches me in the shoulder the way he does every year. I punch him back. "You too, you old bag of fish." We laugh. He says, "I gotta get up for supper. Ma'll skin me if I'm late again. See ya tomorrow, 'kay?" Then, "Howdy, Mr. Merrill. Bye."

Dad and I cross the grassy meadow toward the sea, and up the big sloping rock we call Whaleback. It *is* chilly down here. I stretch out on Whaleback's flat top. It still holds the sun's warmth. The sea is sloshing gently below me. "Remember the year of the hurricane?" I say. "When we stood out here and the waves climbed right up over us? Me, and you and Mom."

Dad nods. We hardly speak of Mom — it's eight months since she died — so it feels big, her name out there on the wind. I shouldn't have mentioned that time, but I feel her so much here. More than at home. I flick a loose stone over the edge of the rock and watch it sink through the clear water.

The beach is different this summer. Not just because Mom's not here. It's different every summer. That's part of what I like about it. Especially the small beach that starts right alongside Whaleback. This year there are way more pebbles washed up, but not so many shells. And a storm has left a spongy mat of seaweed among the rocks that separate the small beach from the big one, where I saw Ian and Zooks earlier.

From the other side of Whaleback, the shoreline is all rocks. On what looks like the far end of it but isn't, sits the Fish House. My family's never used it as a fish house, but somebody did, years ago. It's shaped like a little kid's idea of "a house", and outlined by the white paint on its trim. There's a square white door in the middle of the wall facing Whaleback with a tall rectangular window above it.

Nestled between the rocks and the woods sloping up from the shore, the Fish House has an aura of mystery about it. Only once did anything really mysterious happen there, the time a body washed up that was never identified. But it's where Ian and I went to try out smoking cigarettes when we were twelve and it's where I made the collage for Gran's seventieth birthday that's hanging up in the house.

So it feels like a place for secrets.

Jill

Bees are buzzing in the thistles beside the old barn. Like they're guarding the entrance. But the Merrills are definitely at the house and their car doors are locked. The barn's my only hope. Not that it looks in any better shape than the house out on the point. It doesn't. It's the same dusty grey and its cedar shingles are curling. Some of them have fallen off. Rotting boards only partly cover a space that used to be a window.

Inside the barn there's straw and bird droppings. In the middle of the floor, a stubborn thistle's growing beside a thick coil of rope and an overturned bucket of rusty bolts and springs. Several seasons' worth of abandoned nests droop in the rafters. Hmh. I'm not likely to be bothered by anyone in here.

A small door in the end of the barn swings gently closed. It taps crookedly against its wooden frame. The door begins to swing lazily open again. Is someone there? I step backward into the shadows of the near corner, trip, and crack through the brittle bottom of an old crate.

I squeeze my eyes shut and clench my teeth. I hug my grazed arm against my side. Again, the gentle tap of that door. Who's there? I open my eyes.

The thistle throws back its head as if it's laughing at the stupid girl in the corner. Slowly the door drifts open again. "Wind," laughs the thistle. "No one but wind visits in here."

I pull myself up from the clutter of crates. I kick the one I've broken through. Above there's a flapping of wings against a window.

My arm stings. It's not bleeding much, but I should cover it, or something.

A doorway leads into another room with a single tiny window in the end. It's even dingier in here. And the smell of rotting hay closes in on me like the darkness.

I look out the smeary window. There's two people walking over the hill toward the house. I can't see them too well, but there's a man with his arm around a boy who's almost as tall as him. His son probably.

Must be nice to have a father like that.

It takes a minute for my eyes to get used to the dimness again. In with the straw there's a few broken wooden chairs and rusty lumps of farm machinery. A bent wire gate and an old headboard and bed frame are leaning under the window. Wedged between them there's a mattress with its insides spilling out.

I wad a handful of musty stuffing against the long stinging graze on my arm, then tear at the rotting mattress fabric and wrap it around the stuffing to hold it in place. I park my butt on a pile of boards in the corner. My arm feels better now the air's off it. It's just a graze really, so by morning it should be okay.

Again the panicked flutter of wings from somewhere higher in the barn. It sounds closer now. I look up, into the underside of a set of stairs.

I start up them. The bird begins to swoop back and forth. I pause and the bird comes to rest. I venture a little farther. The bird bee-lines it to the window and again bats its wings against the pane. I sit down near the top of the stairs.

The window next to the bird has no glass in it. It could get out there easy. But no, it's going to bash itself silly trying to go out the wrong way. Stupid bird.

Chad

Gran fries up a sizzling batch of fresh cod and onions for our supper. Dad and I do the cleaning up after. Gran fusses about it not being right that we clean up on our first night here, but we do it anyway. When the dishes are away and the table wiped, and when Dad has refolded the dishcloth I've lumped behind the tap and has hung it neatly at the side of the sink, I suggest a game of Making Words and Taking Words. Gran clasps her hands together like an excited kid.

I find the flannel bag of Scrabble tiles under a handful of shells in the drawer of the sewing machine.

"Your mother always loved Making Words and Taking Words, didn't she, Chad," Gran says.

I've been thinking the same thing, and it strikes me like it did on the way to the beach. I guess I've started getting used to it at home, but being here it's like starting all over again. Everywhere I go, everything I do, something brings her to mind.

"Are you going to play, Gramp?" I ask as we turn the tiles face down on the kitchen table.

"I'll play this part," he says, turning over a few tiles. "It's the only part of this silly game I'm any good at."

"That's 'cause you only try to make words out of the middle," I explain. "You've got to watch the words people have already made —"

"Whuh?"

"I said you've got to watch the words people have already made so you can add letters to them and steal them for yourself."

"I'm too old to learn to look in four different places at once," Gramp grumbles.

But he plays anyway, turning over a letter whenever his turn comes round.

The first letter turned over is an *a*, then a *t*, an *l*, a *k*, then an *e*. Gran and Dad shout at the same time. "Talk." "Late."

"You got it, dear," says Gran, and Dad scoops up the tiles, leaving the *k* in the middle of the table. He lays out L-A-T-E in front of him.

The game goes on and soon Gran shouts, "Pleat."
She scoops up Dad's L-A-T-E and a *p* from the middle
and arranges P-L-E-A-T in front of her.

More words get made and more words get taken.
Gramp and I still have no words. There's a *t*, an *h*, and
and an *e* in the middle of the table, and I blurt out,
"Palette. Sorry, Gran." I slide her P-L-E-A-T over to my
place, take the *t* and the *e* from the middle, to make
P-A-L-E-T-T-E.

"Shouldn't that have two *l*'s?" asks my dad.

"A straw mattress," answers Gramp, "has two *l*'s
and one *t*. Where a painter mixes colours has one *l*,
two *t*'s, and an *e*." Gramp's not much good at putting
together words in this game, but he's considered as
good as the Oxford Dictionary when it comes to
settling arguments about spelling.

"Have you done much painting lately, dear?" Gran
asks me.

In the second I hesitate, Dad jumps in. "It's been
very difficult since Emily's accident. She was quite an
inspiration."

There's not much point, if Dad thinks I've quit, in
telling him about the work I've done at school, or how
much I'm looking forward to painting here at
Dutchman's Bay again. With my luck he'll think we
ought to paint together.

Then Gramp says, "It's just as well if Chad has given it up. It was all very well for Emily to indulge in her painting, but a young man really ought to pursue something more —" I think he's going to say "manly" because Gramp is a bit of a male chauvinist, but he finishes "— more secure."

I'm glad I kept quiet. I don't want to get into justifying my future plans with Gramp. He made it big as a lawyer and is proud of Dad's professorship. He obviously wouldn't think much of his grandson being a painter.

"That may well be," Gran agrees, "but painting can make a lovely hobby too. I hope you'll get back to it some day, Chad."

I nod. "Whose turn is it?"

As if I'm not already sorry enough I made my dumb word, Dad says, "Maybe we could go into Liverpool tomorrow and pick up some brushes and paints, take them down to the beach. I don't know much about it, but we could have fun. Eh, Chad?"

I just shrug and say it's his turn. A few more letters are turned over, a few more words are called. I sit there, praying Dad will forget his awful idea. I have enough trouble getting the effects I want sometimes without him hovering around trying to help. Or just being there. The way he's been bugging me lately, that would be enough to wreck my concentration. I can't let it happen.

"Te-le-path-y," Gramp says slowly.

"What?" His voice brings me back to the game.

"It's my word," Gramp explains. "T-E-L-E-P-A-T-H-Y."
He pulls an *h* and a *y* toward him from the middle of
the table. "Pass me your PALETTE, Chad. I think I've got
the hang of this now."

Jill

I don't know if that stupid bird ever did get out.
It's dark now and I can't see. I think it's sleeping in
the rafters. Something's making little scritchy noises
up there anyway. I lie still, trying to ignore the strange
sounds and mouldy straw smells. The tapping of the
door below feels more hollow and heavier than it did
this afternoon.

When I say it's dark in here, I mean black dark,
not grey dark like my room in Halifax.

I hate that room.

You'd think curled up on the straw in this musty
old barn, I'd be thinking how wonderful my room at
home is, wouldn't you? But not if you saw where we
live now. For one thing my room's about the size of
the closet in my old bedroom. In the house we lived
in in Vancouver. That's probably an exaggeration, but
when your dad screws up and you gotta live on the
peanuts your mom makes waiting tables it's no palace
you can afford to live in, let me tell you. Not that we
lived in a palace in Vancouver, but it was nice. Not like
the dump we live in now.

When Dad got fired 'cause of some heavy duty thing to do with company money, they said we were moving to Halifax. But Halifax has a harbour and water. You can smell the sea there. The little hellhole we ended up in might as well be in the middle of the desert for all you can smell of the sea. And our apartment's so dinky, I'm lucky I've even got a room of my own.

It's a two-bedroom and Mark's got one and I've got the other. My parents sleep on a pull-out in the living room. Mostly Dad. Ma works. She's got two waitressing jobs, she cleans house for this rich family, plus she takes care of us. Not as good as she used to though, and she hates that. Dad on the other hand just dreams a lot, about making it big for his family some day.

At least that's what I thought, till I overheard them fighting this morning. I don't know why Ma doesn't just dump him, but she says marriage is forever, for better or worse. Well, worse is sure what things have got.

It was bad when Mark told them about Amy. Dad wanted Ma to give Mark money so Amy could have an abortion, but she wouldn't. She said it's probably not even his baby. She thinks Mark ought to just stay out of it and Amy ought to give the baby up for adoption. She's on him all the time about not quitting school. I can see why. That's why she has such crumby jobs, 'cause she didn't get any training. I guess she didn't figure on my dad screwing up like he did. But Mark probably won't have to quit school if he can get extra hours at the gas station. And Amy has a good job at Sobey's. She'll work there as long as she can, and they'll take her back after the baby too. So really, Ma should just back off.

But instead she's on me all the time. Ever since Mark told her about Amy she's sure I've been doing it with Jeff too. Just 'cause we hang around a lot together. I could tell her Jeff's not that big a deal to me, and I'd only want to do it with somebody special – I'm kind of old-fashioned that way, I guess, and a bit of a romantic – but what's it to her? Besides, she probably wouldn't believe me.

That's not the worst though. Not only has Dad. . . .

There's a new sound in the blackness around me. Something's moving. A whisper in the bushes and the grass beside the barn. A cool draft steals in through the cracks between the barn boards. The wind, of course, the wind in the grass and in the trees.

But wind doesn't snap branches. Wind doesn't snuffle and rub against a building so you can almost feel its fur.

I try to focus on sounds farther away. A softer version of the crashing waves that lured me into staying too long out on the point. A soothing sound. Like when I was little, growing up in Vancouver.

But I lie awake, my eyes open wide against the black.

Chad

Tangy night air washes into my room, across from Dad's and down the hall from Gran and Gramp's. I push the window open a little higher. The more of Dutchman's Bay I can bring in the better. That's why there are all kinds of shells and starfish and sea urchins lined up on the windowsill and scattered on the dresser. And chunks of gnarled driftwood in the corner – I never get tired of studying their grain lines and the cool shapes they make when you look at them from different angles.

I hoist my duffel bag onto my bed. I'm stuffing clothes into the drawers of my dresser when Dad pokes his head in. "Can I give you a hand with anything, Chad?"

"No thanks, Dad. I'm almost done."

"Let me get you some hangers," he insists and comes back a minute later.

"Thanks." I won't use them. There are pegs in the back of my door if I need to hang anything up. We say goodnight, and I close my door, shoving a lobster buoy in front of it so it won't swing open.

I stick the hangers in the bottom of the dresser and set my Walkman and tapes on the old fish box beside my bed. From the bottom of my duffel bag I take out a photo of my mom and the long wooden box I know she would have wanted me to have. I glance at the closed door and sit on the floor between my bed and the wall.

I cup the photo in my hand. Mom's eyes look up at me, with that look that always meant she was seeing something other people probably didn't see at all. Her cheekbones are high, her chin long. Her mouth looks like she's just starting to smile at some kind of private joke. People always said how much alike we looked. "You'd have a hard time giving him away, Emily," my aunt said more than once. "He's your spitting image," she said, "your spitting image." Mom's hair is long in the picture, the same light brown as mine. She had it cut short not long before the accident, so I guess we looked even more alike then.

I run my hand over the smooth box in my lap. Oak, Mom said, it brought her luck. I slip her photo under the tea towel Gran has laid out on my fish box night table. I glance behind me at the door again before I undo the clasps and open the lid of the box.

The tubes of paint are lined up in a row, the coloured labels all face up. Dioxazine Purple, Alizarin Crimson – it's like having a rainbow in a box, only more – French Ultramarine Blue, Hooker's Green Dark, Cadmium Yellow. All mine to play with how I want. I take the largest of the three brushes from the space above the paints. Mom used these the day of the accident. I stroke the bristles across the palm of my hand.

"I won't let you down, Mom," I whisper.

Saturday

Jill

Birds flap and shriek. A maze. Which way? A mother holds a little girl's hand, leads her away from the birds.

Cold. I reach for my blanket. Not there. Itchy. I scratch. Stiff. I move a little. My bed is so hard. Covered with straw. What happened to my bed? The birds. Not a dream.

I open my eyes. Two birds. I blink. Two barn swallows are on the beam above me talking to each other. And I remember.

I'm in the barn. Trespassers Will Be Prosecuted.

Chad

Usually when I wake up at Dutchman's Bay, I lie in bed for a while and watch the light and shadows change in my room. But today I've got to get up, to make the most of the time before anyone else is up and around.

I throw off the covers and step onto the cotton mat beside my bed. The sun has barely risen and it's caught behind what's left of the night fog. Shivering,

I pull on my jeans and sweatshirt. Carefully I move the wooden buoy away from my door and listen. There's no sound from Dad's darkened room (he shuts his curtains even if there's nobody around for miles), and from Gran and Gramp's, only a soft snoring. I get my runners and the long thin oak box and paper from under my bed, tiptoe out of my room and down the stairs.

There's a jar under the kitchen sink. I fill it slowly, letting the water trickle silently down its side. A swig of milk from the carton in the fridge and a handful of chocolate chip cookies in my pocket, then out I go. I'll put my shoes on outside on the steps.

The sun breaking through the lifting fog makes the Old Barn across the pasture look two-dimensional. Our neighbour's sheep grazing on the hills look like cardboard props for a country stage set.

I head across the field, opposite to the way you'd go to the beach. It's strange to be out before anyone else is up. A sudden movement of birds fluttering out of the bay bushes and alders startles me – I'm edgier than I thought about this.

Jill

One window's cracked, the other's got no glass at all. It's not dark any more. It must be morning.

I brush the straw off my jacket and pick bits of it out of my hair. The birds start flapping around. I hope the stupid things aren't going to go beating against the cracked window again. In two single swoops, they fly out the empty one.

The barn's on a hill, closer to the sea than I realized when I got here last night, just as it was getting dark. The dewy grass and bushes glisten. Mist rising from the sea makes the whole scene look like something out of a fairy tale. Even the ordinary Maritime farmhouse and the ordinary sheep grazing on the hills look magical somehow.

Maybe that's why, when the boy I saw with his father last night saunters across the field, he reminds me of a prince.

That sounds bizarre, I know. Because he's just wearing blue jeans and a dark green sweatshirt and running shoes, like any ordinary guy. He's also popping something into his mouth, which reminds me how hungry I am. Whatever he's eating, I wish I had some.

I rummage around in my knapsack. But when I tossed in a few clothes yesterday, I was expecting to be at Sheila's in time for supper, around the big table in the photos she was always showing off, with her family that actually likes spending time together. So naturally I've got nothing to eat.

And I can't show up at Sheila's for breakfast. Her parents would never believe I got a bus down from Halifax that early in the morning. They'd figure something was fishy, and there's no way I'm telling anybody about this little side-trip. People think I'm stupid enough without giving them proof. Not that it's my fault I'm here or anything. But still.

I stand up to look out the window again. I feel dizzy. I can't make it to Sheila's anyway. Not without getting something to eat.

The boy's disappearing into the woods. I could follow him. He'd probably give me some of what he's got.

Yeah, right. You're going to go up to this guy you never met, right out of the blue, and say, "Excuse me, I'm a little hungry 'cause I was too stupid to find my friend's place in time for dinner last night. Would you mind sharing what you're eating with me?" And he's going to say, "Why certainly, miss, take all I have. Then I'll give you a lift to your friend's in my parents' BMW."

More likely he'd say, "Can't you read? The sign says no trespassing. Beat it, before I report you to the police."

Besides, he's probably already wolfed down everything he had. The pig.

But since when do I have to depend on some guy? Even if he does look like a prince. There's more food where his came from. A whole kitchenful.

Chad

Once I'm into the green canopy of the woods I begin to relax. I feel more protected. From what I don't know. My dad suddenly waking up and following me, I guess.

The mossy ground slopes downward. The background roar of the sea grows gradually louder. I step out of the woods and a crash of waves on the rocks greets me. That and the salty seashore smell. I can taste the mist on my lips.

It's the kind of day Mom loved. Not sunny and clear the way most people like. All misty and grey. The fog is lifting enough so I can just make out Whaleback Rock along the shore, and in patches, the beach beyond it. There's a brightness to the haze. It probably won't be long before the sun burns it off. I wish Mom was here.

I clamber over the rocks to the Fish House, pause on the step, then pull at the heavy wooden door. Swollen in the damp it barks like a seal as it opens.

Inside, the Fish House looks like it always does. There's an old fish box at the window facing the sea, where people sit and look out. Navigation charts of the coastal area are tacked on the back wall. There's a tattered ancient fish net draped in the corner, a few wooden buoys like the one in my room, a rusty fish jack, and a ladder with a broken rung. I close the door behind me.

No one uses the upper level of the Fish House. The ladder is rotting and the floor is weak in spots. No one's been up there for ages.

I kick the cobwebs from the wooden ladder lying under the maps and lean it into the hole in the upper floor. I test each rung on the way up to be sure it'll still take my weight.

The floor up here is uneven. An old piece of driftwood, just right for a seat, waits by the window at the far end of the room.

Rock upon rock upon rock stretch around the shoreline, rust and pink, yellow, black, white. Rounded boulders tumble into the sea like petrified dinosaur eggs. There are jagged outcroppings of granite among them. The shoreline curves in a widening strip of sand beach then becomes rocky again at the next point, still hidden in the mist.

I run my hand over the smooth oak box I took from Mom's studio before the movers Dad arranged came to clear it out. I haven't painted as much as usual this year, Dad's right about that, and what I have done hasn't been very good. I've never been as good as Mom, not nearly, but I want to be. She'd like that. And it would be like I'm keeping her with me, in a way.

She was proud of me, gave me all that encouragement. Being here at Dutchman's Bay again will help me get back into it.

Jill

My knees are like rubber going down the barn stairs. I lean against the doorframe. The field and trees in the lifting fog won't hold steady. I slide down to the beam across the bottom of the doorway to catch my breath. But I don't have much time. The house looks asleep — don't ask me how I can tell, it just does — but it probably won't be for long. And that guy might come back.

The heads of the bobbing thistles and wild carrot dance in front of my face. Sorry, I'm not applauding your lousy performance today. I take a deep breath, stand slowly.

At the edge of the field I crouch in the bushes, watching the house for signs of life.

The sheep stop grazing. It feels like they're waiting to see what I'm going to do. Swallows swoop from one hydro wire to another. They're talking. About me probably. *She's going to steal. Do you believe it? She's never done this before. She'll get caught for sure.*

I nervously tear a leaf from one of the bushes, roll it between my hands, and am surprised at the fresh spicy smell. Stupid, bayleaf has to grow *somewhere*.

I won't get caught. Not if the boy's parents are still asleep, and whoever belongs to the other car parked at the back of the house. And if I move fast. And don't make any noise.

That's a lot of ifs.

But what if someone's awake? I listen. Birds. The sea. A sheep bleats. Nothing from inside the house. But what do I expect at dawn — a party?

What if someone's sitting right there when you open the door? I could peek in first. What if they're in the next room? As soon as I step in, they'd catch me. Then what? "Oops, sorry, wrong house."

Hardly. It's not like the door to our apartment, identical to the other five on our floor and the three floors above.

More likely they'd call the cops. And that's just what I need. If it's like the Spanish Inquisition every time I come home now, what'll it be like if I get in trouble with the cops? It's way more likely the people in the house would get that upset than the kid who went into the woods. He might think I'm an idiot, but he's not going to bother calling the cops if all I'm doing's asking for a bite of his cookie. Besides, it's hardly the sort of thing royalty would do, is it?

Chad

What to paint? The whole rocky shoreline disappearing into the mist? Or one of the rocks close up?

One with orange lichens clinging to it maybe, or one with crusty barnacles clustered on its side. Or the rocks farther out? Being low tide, they look like someone has thrown a soggy shag carpet over them. I can't decide.

The rhythm of the sea wraps around the Fish House, rolling to shore in louder and louder waves, then receding, calm, and then building again.

I open the box and look at the rows of coloured tubes, hoping they'll tell me what to paint this morning. I choose a grey, mix it with a lot of water on a large clam shell, and brush it onto the paper. I still haven't decided what I'm painting, but this grey is too dark, whatever it's going to be. I try watering it down, but all I get is a puddley mess.

I take a fresh piece of paper, wipe clean the shell I'm using for a palette. I have an idea now. With a clean brush I stroke water onto the paper, then squish a blob of Purple Madder Alazarin onto the palette, and a blob of Cerulean Blue. I dab the colours onto the paper, but the way they run together isn't right. I try again, but I'm getting nowhere. There's no flow to what's happening, no magic. It's nothing like when I painted here last year.

What ever made me think I can learn to paint as well as my mom and carry on where she left off? She lied about how good I was, trying to make me feel good. This is worse than the crap I've been doing at school. I fling the pad of paper off my lap and slam down the lid of the oak box.

Maybe it's just as well. Like Gramp said last night, it's not a very secure field to go into, for anybody. And just 'cause you want something, want to be something, doesn't mean you can.

I rinse the paint out of the brush, squeeze the bristles between my fingers.

But this can't be the last time I'll feel the wet smoothness of a brush. Or the magic of being lost in a painting. The pattern the running colour is making on the damp paper *is* kind of interesting. I won't give up.

Below me the door rubs open. Dad. I stop breathing. Don't find me here.

He won't. Nobody ever comes up here.

But there's the ladder. He has to see it. Then he'll know.

The sea whispers in my ears for what feels like minutes. I must have been hearing things. No one was awake when I left the house, so how can there be anyone down here now?

The top of the ladder jiggles.

"Hello?" A girl's voice.

I rush to the ladder. Kneeling by the hole, I look down.

She's standing very still, like someone posing for a portrait. She has one hand on the ladder, the other in the pocket of her denim jacket. Her dark brown hair flies loose around her upturned face. Dampness clings to it like mist to a spider web. Her eyes are so dark and so deep, it's like you could fall into them. She's said nothing more than hello. But in her eyes there is sadness, hope, and fear.

"Who are you?"

Jill

As soon as I see the little house perched on the rocks I know it's where I want to stay. Forget Sheila's cottage – it wasn't a real invitation anyway. I just convinced myself it was when I needed somewhere to go.

A crash of waves flattens out on the lumpy seaweed, reaching long arms toward the grey building, then trickling away to get swallowed up by the next wave. Again. And again. The mist's cool on my face. It feels wilder here than where I grew up. Wild, but safe. It feels like where I belong. For as long as I would've stayed at Sheila's, I can stay here.

If I can talk that guy into bringing me food.

Back towards the house and the barn, the rocky shoreline tumbles along the base of a cliff. In the other direction, the land's flatter. Farther along, skeletons of birch trees pose like brittle dancers at the edge of the rocks. There's no sign of him either way. He must've gone into my house.

Okay, I know it's not mine, it's probably his, one of these rich brats with more places to go than they know what to do with. But I need it more than he does, and without even having gone in yet, it feels like mine.

But still, when I stand in front of the heavy wooden door, it feels like I should knock. I guess in spite of how things've been lately, I was brought up right. But I can't imagine any of the people who've climbed this worn step ever knocking.

The door, with its white paint cracked and chipped, sounds like it's got whooping cough when I tug it open and slip inside.

He's not here, it seems, just a bunch of old fishing stuff, and a rickety ladder leaning into a hole in the ceiling. I call up, "Hello?"

His face at the top of the ladder tells me loud and clear he doesn't want me here. Why would he? Kneeling beside the hole, he asks, like he's ready for a fight, "Who are you?" His fair hair, long on the top, flops into his blue eyes.

I put my foot on the first rung. Right away he says, "Don't come up."

I'm going to have to be careful here, if I'm going to get any help from this guy. He starts down the ladder. It creaks and wobbles. He's thin, but not scrawny.

"There's a rung missing," I warn him.

"I know it," he snaps, "how do you think I got up?"

"Well, excuse me. I just didn't want you to fall."

"I'm fine," he says when he reaches the bottom. His full upper lip turns up on one side. He's got a thinker's forehead and a dreamer's eyelashes, like my brother's. He moves the ladder from the hole and lays it against the wall under a bunch of maps. "Who are you?" he repeats. "What are you doing here?"

I should've thought this out better. There must be some way of doing it. Sure, I could turn on the charm. Smelling of old barn and looking like something the cat dragged in, it would do me a lot of good.

"If you're not going to tell me. . . . "

"Jill," I say.

"Jill."

I nod. "I saw you cross the field and go into the woods."

"You followed me here?"

I just nod again. Telling him about my first plan to go steal food out of his kitchen's hardly going to win me any points.

"Why?"

"I'm hungry," I tell him.

"You're hungry?"

Boy, this guy's great at conversation. "Yes, I'm hungry. You had something to eat. I . . . "

"Yeah, I had something to eat and I ate it. Why don't you go home and get your own food? Don't you live around here?"

Oh good. He's smartening up. "You know the barn?" I say. "On the hill back there?"

"Of course. It belongs to my grandparents." He brushes his hair out of his eyes again. "What about it?"

Do I have to spell it out for him? Can't he smell the musty barn in my jacket, and in my hair? Can't he see it? Maybe he's too stupid to help and keep quiet about it too. His eyes drop to my jacket then, and look back at my face. "You slept in the Old Barn?"

"Yeah."

"Why?"

"I made a mistake, okay. I just needed somewhere to stay."

"Have you run away from home or something?" he asks.

"Just 'cause I slept in your lousy barn doesn't mean I owe you my life story. All I want's for you to bring me something to eat."

"Pretty bossy for someone looking for a favour, aren't you?"

"Maybe I should just go back out to the point. There's some guys out there who'd help me without all this hassle."

"What point?"

"Out there," I tell him, pointing along the shore.

"You stayed out at Dead Man's Point?"

"What if I did?" Okay, so I didn't. But this guy won't get off my case, and he's obviously in awe at the thought I might've stayed out there, so I can't help stringing him along.

"The old fisherman who lived there was murdered in that house," he tells me.

"So? I don't believe in ghosts. Do you?"

"No. I just mean, they never found who did it. I — don't think you should hang around out there, that's all."

Outside the window a seagull squawks. It dives to the water and takes off again. Of course, I didn't think I should hang around out there either.

"Go back to the barn," the boy says, "I'll bring you something when I can."

"Why don't I just stay here?"

"You can't. People in my family come down here, our neighbours sometimes too."

I nod and walk to the door. The last wisps of haze are blowing off the point of land across the bay. There's a long sandy curve of beach now that was hidden in the fog when I came down. "What about upstairs?"

"What do you mean?"

"I bet nobody but you bothers going up there. Not judging by the condition of your ladder. Why can't I stay up there? I could pull up the ladder and no one would know."

"It's dangerous."

"You were up there."

"No."

"You being naughty up there?" I tease him.

"Listen, you're the one who doesn't belong here." He shoves his hair off his face. "And you're not staying at Dead Man's again, if you ever did. If you want me to bring you anything, get back to the barn."

Right. Well, he's not as tough as he's trying to act. He just wants me out of here. If I hadn't barged in on some big secret, he'd probably be really getting off on the idea of helping some damsel in distress. Yuck.

But he's right. I don't belong here. Not that his reminding me makes me fall in love with him exactly. But I need something to eat, so I better not push my luck. Let him have his stupid house. I shrug and head toward the woods.

"Don't go the way you came," he calls to me. "Someone might see you. Take that other path. It circles around to the back of the barn, so you don't have to cut across the field."

Crossing the rocks to the other path I call back, "When will you come?"

"When I can."

Chad

There isn't time for any painting once that girl heads back to the barn. She must have run away. I wonder what from. I'll have to try to get back here later. After I've taken the refugee something to eat.

What a pain. Why'd I say I'd do it? But how could I not?

Half a dozen swallows fly in at the broken window of the sagging barn. No way I can imagine sleepingthere. Is this girl in big trouble, nuts, or what? She sure looked scared, till she got so mad. Whatever she's up to, I wish I hadn't agreed to help.

But Mom would be proud. She was always packing our old clothes off to Goodwill, and inviting someone for Christmas dinner if she found out they were going to be alone. "We have so much," she said. "Just because you can't change the world doesn't mean you don't do what you can." I guess that's what I'm doing.

But she better clear out once she's eaten. It'll be hard enough staying out of Dad's way this summer, I don't want to have to worry about *her* hanging around too.

The smells of coffee and bacon waft out the screen door. Inside, sunshine washes over the pale yellow walls.

"Been over to Ian's already?" Dad asks.

"No. Just out."

"At this hour?" He checks his watch and lifts a boiled egg from the pan of water on the stove.

"Can't a guy just go for a walk before breakfast?"

"Certainly," Dad says. "You should have woken me though. I might have come with you."

"Sometimes a person likes to walk alone," says Gramp, "eh, Chad?"

I nod. "Sometimes."

Gran brings a stack of toast that could feed our school's football team out of the oven and sets it in the middle of the table. She moves the jars of marmalade and honey to make room for the plate of bacon. Gramp spoons hot fat over the frying eggs. "These look done," he says. "Would you like me to put one in for you, Chad?"

"Give him one of yours, dear," says Gran. "You shouldn't be eating two eggs."

"You know what the doctor said," Dad says.

Gramp mumbles and serves out the eggs, to Gran and me and himself. He takes a handful of bacon from the plate. "If I'm going to die young, I'm going to die young," he says, and winks at me across the blue checkered table cluttered with food.

Dad sits down with his boiled egg nestled in a china egg cup. With his knife he taps gently around the shell. He slips the knife neatly into the crack, lifts the cap off the egg. He scrapes the cap clean with his spoon and eats the little round circle of white. "Mmhm," he says, as he does every morning at this point in the egg ritual. He sprinkles pepper onto the egg in the cup, three sharp shakes worth. I hardly hear what anyone is saying, his fussy routine drives me so bats. Next time I go to the Fish House I'll try and stay long enough to miss it.

When the egg is eaten he lifts the shell between his thumb and middle finger and scrapes it clean. Then he sets it back in the china egg cup and drops in the shell from the cap. "Mmhm," he says again.

I know, it's dumb to let it bug me so much. What's it matter how a guy eats his egg, right? But you'd sure never see Mom fussing like that over an egg. She was more a dump-it-in-the-pan-and-beat-the-hell-out-of-it type. If she got a bit of shell in it she'd just scoop it out with a finger, if she even noticed it. I know — so what.

"... to do some painting."

"Pardon."

"The paint on the side steps," Dad says, "is starting to peel. Do you think you might find time today to do some painting?"

"Steps." I grin. "Sure." I get up from the table. "I'll start now."

I'm scraping old blue-grey flakes of paint off the steps. Dad and Gramp step outside.

"You're doing a good job there, Chad," Dad says.

"Yeah. Thanks."

"I'm going to go down to the Fish House for a while where it's quiet," Gramp says. It sounds like a funny thing for a guy who doesn't hear much to say, but I know what he means. Gramp shades his eyes with his hand as he looks up at the birds flying on and off the hydro wires, darting across the field. "The barn swallows are certainly excited about something this morning," he says.

That's when I remember the girl, still waiting for something to eat. I keep scraping away at the step, conscious of my dad watching.

Jill

There's nothing to do except wait and watch out this knothole. It's right about eye level when I'm perched on this lobster trap. Not that there's much happening. Prince Whatsisface seems to be having breakfast for an awfully long time. Could it be he actually sits down with his family for meals and pleasant conversation? That'd sure be different from my place, where nobody's ever around at the same time, or has anything to say that wouldn't cause massive indigestion anyway.

It wasn't always like that. Just since my dad screwed up and we had to move. He kept chasing these half-baked schemes that were supposed to make him a bundle and things kind of went from bad to worse. Ma got a job as soon as Dad got laid off or whatever the first time, but it didn't pay much, so she soon took on more work. She's hardly home any more, and Dad — well, he's around alright, but he's such an oaf, why would anybody want to talk to him? Mark's okay, of course, and we still have some good talks, but not sitting down over breakfast or anything.

More likely in my dinky little room. Or eating fritters in the parking lot outside the donut place. Mark's not allowed inside since the fight he had there with some old boyfriend of Amy's. It's not fair, 'cause Mark isn't the type who goes looking for a fight. That other guy was asking for it, saying those things about Amy. The actual fight wasn't all that bad, but a lot of real tough guys do come in there. So, I guess you can't really blame the owner if he doesn't always know which ones he ought to keep out.

Anyway, it was outside this donut place that Mark told me about Amy being pregnant. It's not fair, 'cause they were being real careful. Just this once they forgot. He loves her so much, I bet they would've got married some day anyway. But with the baby coming in November, it's going to be real soon. Ma and Dad have threatened to disown him if he has anything more to do with "this tramp". They never call Amy by her name.

Sure, it's going to be hard for him to finish school after he's married, and a dad, and everything. But he'll do it. I know he will. And if I move in with them, I can help babysit and save them a bunch of money. If Dad hadn't screwed up so bad, Ma could've babysat fulltime and saved them even more.

It probably doesn't sound much like my mom's the babysitting-grandmother type. Well, she *is* real young to be a grandmother. She was only nineteen when she had Mark. But she loves babies, and was a great mother when we were little, reading us books and taking us to the park all the time, stuff like that. Not that she's not still a good mother, but she's tired, and doesn't do so hot at understanding us as she used to.

Like my whole thing with Jeff. I like him and we spend a lot of time together. But she gets so paranoid about us being alone too much, especially since Amy got pregnant. She doesn't get it that we're just friends. Actually, Jeff seems to forget that too sometimes. I mean, we do get a little friendlier than "just friends" once in a while. But nothing much. I don't want anything big to happen till I'm in love. Corny, eh? But that's the way I am. I've tried to tell Ma that, but she must think I'm some kind of weakling or Jeff's some kind of animal or something. All I know is she's on my case all the time about where I'm going, how I'm getting there, who I'll be with, what we'll be doing, when I'll be home, how I'm getting home, and any other stupid thing she can think of.

Wouldn't she get a kick out of this little picnic?

I wish this guy who's supposed to be bringing me food would hurry up and remember I'm out here, hungry and waiting.

He finally does come out of the house, only he's not coming here. He's doing something at the steps.

It's gorgeous out now and I could kick myself for not being at Sheila's. I love this place, but being holed up in the barn is real stupid. I should've just taken my chances earlier and raided the kitchen myself.

A few minutes later two men come out of the house. The older one heads across the field, very slowly, the grandfather who owns this place probably. The one who must be the father stays and talks to his son, helping him too, it looks like.

Yesterday when I saw them walking over the hill together, I thought it was kind of neat. I guess it still is. But for some reason it really chafes me this morning. Partly 'cause I'm hungry, and wonder if this jerk's forgotten me, but also it's such a startling reminder of what my dad isn't.

I've been trying not to think about him, my dad, but he's actually the reason I decided to escape to Sheila's for a while. It's not just that it ticks me off to see him lying around the apartment all the time when Ma's out working. It's what I just found out yesterday that was — what do people call it? — the last straw.

See, I've known for a long time that my dad got fired 'cause he cheated the company he was working for out of a pile of money, and that made it kind of hard for him to get hired anywhere else, except for dumpy kinds of places where they don't much care what kind of crook you are. Actually I guess even the dumpy places don't want you around if you're a crook. Any other kind of bum maybe, but not a crook.

Finding that out was bad, but Dad's a real sweet-talker, so I more or less bought it when he cried and said he just did it 'cause he wanted the best for his family. But months went by, and it stopped looking like he cared about getting another job at all. Even my mom started to wonder how hard he was trying, but he always managed to convince her how difficult it was, the economy's bad, all that stuff. She stayed sucked in by him longer than I did.

We've had a couple of real doozie fights about it too, 'cause I told her she ought to just dump him, 'cause he's a crook and a slob. Of course she said that was "no way to talk about my father" (even if it was true), and gave me a big lecture about marriage being forever, for better or worse, and all that. The thing is, I agree, but only to a point. And if things hadn't reached that point before this week, they sure have now.

One thing my mom's worked hard to make sure I can still have is my dance classes. I started them when I was little, just like a million other kids. I also started gymnastics and swimming and drama and T-ball and hockey and guitar. But dancing's what I stuck with and Ma knows how important it is to me.

Not that I just sit back and take whatever she hands me. I help out. Almost everything I make babysitting goes into my dancing — shoes or classes or something. And believe me, I've taken a few jobs I'd have been happy to turn down too.

Anyway, Ma put something out of almost every paycheque and pocketful of tips into this separate account, so when the fees for the next session were due, the money'd be there.

Well, yesterday morning Ma and Dad had this whopping fight. I don't mean he hit her or anything – he hasn't stooped that low yet. But he'd cleaned out the account that had my dancing money in it. Ma was livid. I've never seen her so mad. Actually I still haven't. I've just heard it. There was no way I was coming out of my room while this one was going on.

Turns out he thought he could put the money back 'cause of some "sure thing". He took it, "borrowed" it he says, 'cause he knew he could put it back and way more, when this "sure thing" paid off. Eventually I figured out this "sure thing" was some horse. He lost the money on some stupid bet. From what Ma was saying, it wasn't the first time. I don't know how long she knew for, but she sure did a good job keeping it from me and Mark. At least, I don't think he knows. He would've told me if he did.

Anyway, this is the kind of guy my dad is. So it's no big surprise if it gets to me that this kid, who's already eaten an undoubtedly humungous breakfast, also has this together father. I know just 'cause they went for a walk and he's working on the steps with him doesn't mean he might not be some kind of creep, but a father who's that interested in spending time with his kid isn't about to go stealing from him. That's for sure.

Chad

Dad presses one of the steps with his fingers. "This board is starting to rot," he says. "It doesn't make much sense to paint a rotting board."

I drop the scraper onto the grass.

"It would be worth the effort to replace it," he continues, "if we could find an extra board around somewhere."

"In the barn," I almost shout. "Isn't there some wood in there from when you and — from when you were planning to rebuild the floor of the Fish House?"

"That's right. Let's go see what's there."

"No, Dad. It's okay. Let me go." I head up the steps into the house. "You take a turn on the scraping. You're so much more careful about it than I am."

"Okay," Dad says, "but where are you going now?"

"I need to grab a bite to eat."

"Hungry already, Chad? You just finished breakfast."

"A guy builds up an appetite," I insist, "working in the sun."

Fortunately Gran is upstairs, whistling about something, so I'm free to raid the pantry without arousing any more suspicion. I shove a few chocolate chip cookies into my pocket. What else? She needs more than a few cookies. There are some crusts of bread in a bag in the bread box. I tuck that inside my shirt — it's good it's baggy — along with a banana from the fruit bowl. I also grab an apple, which I take a bite of and wave at my dad.

"Sure you don't want some help with the wood?" he asks.

"I'll holler if I need you, 'kay?"

The barn is silvery grey against the cobalt sky, about a football field's length away from the house. I cross the field through the bay bushes, squinting now and then to make the sunny leaves brighter and the shadows darker. I brush past the thistles in the doorway.

In the middle of the floor a single thistle is growing. Its purple head and green leaves are vivid against the dirt. It would make a dynamite painting.

I kick aside a broken crate and step into the other room, darker and mustier. The boards will be under the stairs. But first, the girl — I've forgotten her name. "Hello?" I whisper.

"Up here," she says softly.

I climb the stairs into the loft. A bird swoops back and forth through the room.

The girl is sitting on a lobster trap under the cracked and broken windows. She raises her dark eyes. "I thought you weren't coming." At the sound of her voice, the bird settles in the rafters.

"I said I would, didn't I?"

"I saw you working on the steps. Is that your dad?"

I look out the window. Dad's bent over, scraping. Gran's behind the house, hanging some washing on the line. "Yeah."

"What did you bring?"

I shake the bread and banana from under my shirt and hand them to her. And the apple and the cookies in my pocket.

She rips the peel off the banana. Four bites and it's gone. She looks at the other stuff. "Is this all?"

"You should be glad you got this," I tell her. "If I didn't have to come here for a board, I don't know when I could have got away."

She shrugs, and mumbles something with her mouth full. Her fingernails are dirty. Her eyelashes are dark and long.

I look away. There are spaces between the darkened barn boards, and knotholes where the sun beams in. Dusty straw is heaped up in the corner, where I guess she slept last night. What she's run away from must be bad, or else what she's done is bad enough she wants to be sure she doesn't get caught.

"It was good of you to do this for me." The girl raises her eyes from the bread she's eating. Her eyes. When she looks at me it's hard to let go.

But through the window above her I catch that Dad's coming this way. No doubt to help me with the wood. "I've got to go," I tell her, crossing the tiny room to the stairs. "My dad's coming across the field." The girl presses her face to the wall. When she looks back at me I see the knothole. I guess she's been spying on us all morning. And last night? Yesterday?

"I'll go soon," she says, "when the coast looks clear."

"You better."

I'm on the stairs when she asks my name.

I tell her, "Chad. Sshh," and hurry down.

"Thank you, Chad," she whispers.

Jill

Chad, eh? What's that short for? Chadwick? Chaddley? Chadderton? Not Chadderbox, that's for sure. I know — Chadpole. Chadpole Frudruck Merrill — The Fifth.

I've slid off the lobster trap so I can watch through a crack between the floorboards. Boy, is Chad's father ever different. His clothes are so neat, his Eddie Bauer T-shirt all tucked in. And he's shaved. Even though he's on holidays.

My dad never shaved on holidays, a long time ago I mean, when he still had a job to take holidays from. He grew a beard, every summer, then shaved it off again when holidays were over. But I loved it when he had his beard. On the way over to our cottage, on the ferry, he'd laugh and rub his sandpaper face against my cheek. By the time we were heading back home it was easier to snuggle up to him and it tickled when I kissed him. I loved to bury my fingers in the soft thickness of it. That was when I was really little.

There's nothing special about his beard now. It's just another sign of how lazy he is.

I hunch real still over the crack while they're down below, checking through the stack of boards. Chad sounds kind of stiff talking to his father, probably 'cause he knows I'm listening. The straw dust on the floor tickles my nose. I have to squeeze it so I don't sneeze. When finally they've decided on a board — boy, is his dad picky — and Chad is right underneath me, I brush a little dust over the edge of a crack in the floor, just enough for it to trickle down onto Chad's neck. I have to cover my mouth so I don't laugh.

I start to watch Chad and his father crossing the field with the board. But this is my chance to get away. I shove my jacket into my knapsack, head down the stairs, and with a quick glance back at Chad and the sea, head up to the road.

I kick a stone, then run to catch up to it. I kick it again and watch it tumble along the gravel and into the raspberry bushes growing by the ditch. I cup my hand under the dark red berries and tap them into it. Soon my hand is full. I tip them into my mouth, feel their tart juiciness explode there.

I haven't gone far when a truck rattles up behind me. As if I've been doing it all my life, I turn and stick out my thumb. It's hot and dry and I'm anxious to get to Sheila's where I can be by the sea again and get a proper meal.

The blue pick-up stops just ahead. It's hard to believe it was only yesterday I hitched for the first time, when I was supposedly leaving Halifax by bus. That's what I told Ma anyway, that if I took the bus to Liverpool, Sheila's parents could pick me up there. It wasn't a lie exactly. They could've picked me up there if I'd taken the bus, if they knew I was coming, if Sheila and I'd made more of a plan than, "You should come some time" – "Maybe I will."

"Where to?" The rumpled driver smells of fish and cigarette smoke.

I roll down my window a few inches. "Just out to the highway, thanks. Or up to the next road if you're going that way?"

"Heading down to Yarmouth myself," the guy says. "I'll drop you before I turn down. Cigarette?" He nods at the open pack on the dashboard.

"No thanks."

He reaches across to the glovebox. I put my hand on the door handle, ready to jump. A chocolate bar lies on top of a jumble of papers and I laugh. Stupid.

"Like chocolate?"

I nod.

"Take it."

I've eaten half the bar before it occurs to me to offer him a piece. But he grins at me with a few brown teeth and shakes his head. A few minutes later he pulls up at the Irving. I thank him for the lift, and the chocolate bar, and bang shut the rusty door.

The familiar red IRVING on the white circle above the gas pumps reminds me I still don't know if Mark knows where I am. Well, not where exactly, but that I headed for Sheila's yesterday. Will he have talked to Ma? There's a phone booth beside the store near the gas station. Maybe he'll be home now.

If someone else answers, I'll say I forgot to call yesterday to say I arrived. It won't be a lie if I don't say where.

The phone rings, eight rings. "I'm sorry," says the operator. "Your number is not answering." I hang up, dial another number, and go through the collect call stuff with the operator again. This time there's an answer.

"Charlotte, it's me."

"Jill, where are you? I thought . . . "

"Excuse me," interrupts the operator, "this is a collect call from Jill Croft, do you accept the charge?"

"Yes, it's Jill!"

"I'm thrilled," the operator says.

"Charlotte, I didn't get a chance to talk to Mark yesterday. If you see him, can you tell him I'm at Sheila's? I don't want him to worry about me."

"Where are you, Jill? I know you're not at Sheila's."

"What do you mean?"

"Sheila came home from her cottage yesterday afternoon. Her parents are splitting up." Charlotte drones on while I try to take in what this means. "So, what's going on? Jill, are you there?"

"Charlotte, do my parents know about Sheila?"

"Your mom was on her way out to work when the Merritts drove up. When Sheila didn't know where you were, your mom called me."

"What'd you tell her?"

"What could I tell her? I thought you were gone to Sheila's too. I don't think she believed me. Where are you, Jill?"

"It doesn't matter." Of course my mother didn't believe her. Just like she'll never believe another word I say.

"Your mom's real worried, Jill. She went down to the police station when you still weren't there when she got home from work."

What've I done? She'll never let me out of her sight.

"Charlotte, do you know where I can get a hold of Mark? Do you have the number at the Irving?"

"He won't be there. Oh, but you don't know, do you."

"What?" The stuffiness of the phone booth's almost smothering me.

"Mark and Amy took off," Charlotte says. "He finally had it with all your parents' lousy ultimatums. They've gone to some aunt's of hers. Somewhere up near Antigonish."

I swallow hard and focus on the waves of heat rippling off the highway, my choices evaporating. I lean against the dusty wall of the phone booth. Charlotte's words garble on, telling me only one thing.

I can't go home.

"Charlotte," I interrupt, "don't tell anyone I called. I gotta go." I slam down the phone, lean my throbbing head against it.

Yeah, I've gotta go. But where?

Chad

Dust is trickling onto my neck. I take a swipe at it, like it's a pesky insect before I realize. At first it really bugs me she'd take that kind of chance, after the trouble I went to. But then I find myself fighting back a smile — you know, the way you sometimes can't help laughing at the class goof pulling some stunt to get the teachers going.

I'm tempted to turn around when Dad and I are crossing the field back to the house, as if she might be making funny faces at the window or something, but I don't want to draw Dad's attention that way, if this is when she's making her getaway. Getaway — makes her sound like some kind of criminal. Is she? How'd she end up in our Old Barn? Where's she off to next? I guess I'll never know.

It doesn't take long to pry off the rotting board, to cut the new one to the right length, and to bang it in. Dad insists on sanding down the rough edges of old paint. The steps aren't really big enough for two people to work at, so I'm glad when Gran calls Dad in to help her with something.

I'm stroking on the new paint in long even strokes when a shadow crosses the steps. My first thought is that girl. But she's long gone by now.

"They going to keep you working all summer?" It's Ian.

I shrug. "Painting's not work." I dip the brush into the can again, and stroke shiny grey-blue along the fresh wood.

"I heard you banging at something a while ago," objects Ian. "Don't tell me that wasn't work."

"I guess." I wipe the sweat from my forehead. "Want to go down to the beach when I'm done?"

"Sure thing. It'll be our only chance this summer."

"What are you talking about? We go down there almost every day."

"Not this year. I got me a job. I'll be gone six weeks. I leave after lunch."

It's not such a big deal, but it gets to me. I guess 'cause I've known Ian since we were ankle-biters, carrying our buckets down to the beach with our moms till we were old enough to go ourselves, then taking sandwiches out to Picnic Point. One summer we used the Old Barn for a clubhouse, and hid there for hours when his geeky cousin came to stay while her parents went away to decide if they should still be married. And then there's all the hours we spent riding the surf on styrofoam boards, exploring along the rocks, finding neat stuff like broken boats and once a dead seal, building enormous castles in the sand and watching the tide come in and wash them away, hiking out to Dead Man's Point. Ian's been a major part of my summers here.

It's dumb, but the only thing I can think of to say is, "I'll miss you."

"Sorry, kid," Ian says, "but what can I do? My old man says if I'm not going to school any more, it's time I started paying my own way around here."

"You're not going back to school in the fall?"

"What for? I'm sixteen now. I'm ready to live."

The way he says it makes me feel suddenly like Ian's left me way behind, that I'm ages younger than him instead of just four months. For one thing, I figure on being in school for a long time yet, finishing high school, going on to university, maybe even art college, although only my mom knew I was thinking about that. For another — I can't put my finger on it. He just seems — older.

"I thought I heard your voice out here, Ian," Gran says through the screen. "You're just the man I wanted."

"Don't open the door, Gran," I say. "The paint's wet."

"Yes, I can see that, dear. Ian, I have a bit of a problem in here. Would you mind coming in and having a look at it for me?"

"For you, sweetheart?" Ian replies. "Anything."

Gran smiles like a school-girl, a pink blush spreading up her cheeks. Ian leaps to his feet and saunters round to the front door.

That Ian. Such a charmer. Even with Gran.

Under the blazing sun, I go back to painting the steps. Slowly. To the rhythm of the lazy sea below the hills and beyond. Dip. Stroke. Stroke. Stroke. Then again, dip. Stroke. I can feel my back starting to burn, stop to pull on my T-shirt, then go back at it again.

Finally the last of the wood disappears under the glossy paint. I go in and grab a Coke from the fridge.

Ian is wiping his greasy hands on some newspaper. "That should fix it," he says.

"Thank you, so much, Ian," Gran says. "Would you like a cup of coffee?"

It strikes me Gran's never offered me coffee, and it hits me wrong. Standing there with my can of Coke, I feel like somebody's kid brother hanging around where he doesn't belong. Which is dumb, 'cause I'd rather have Coke than coffee any day.

Ian doesn't want a coffee either, so we head off as soon as he washes the rest of the grease from the sewing machine motor off his hands.

Out on the hill he says, "I was sorry to hear about your mom," I guess to kind of give me a chance to talk about her if I want. People do that a lot I've noticed, but I don't really have much to say.

I end up telling Ian instead about how I used to run for the cross-country school team so every morning I got up and ran, and how not long after Mom died, Dad thought it would be nice for us to run together. It seemed to mean a lot to him, and I didn't know how to say I didn't want to without hurting his feelings. But it was hopeless. Every morning he puffed along beside me and I had to slow down for him to keep up. He always wanted to chat about the situation with Quebec or whether I was going to join the math club or something. And who cares, right? All I wanted to do was run.

"So, why didn't you tell him?" Ian asks.

"I should have. He even said once, You run ahead if you want. Don't let your old man slow you up. — I don't know why but his saying it like that made it impossible. I ended up not even going to the final track meet, I was so out of shape from not getting a proper workout."

Ian laughs. "You're too nice a guy for your own good."

"I don't know why just 'cause my mom's gone, he thinks I need *him* around all the time."

"Maybe he's lonely."

"Yeah, I guess I kind of figured that. That's what makes it so hard to tell him to get lost. Besides," I say, "my dad's a nice guy. I just wish he'd give me a little space, that's all."

"Parents don't like to do that unless you make them," Ian says, and sounds like he knows what he's talking about. If he's taken a job that gets him away from home for six weeks I guess he does. I have to admire his doing that, like some part of me admired the nerve of that girl hiding in our barn, asking me to feed her, then just – moving on. Even with how I've been feeling about my dad lately, I can't imagine making the kind of break Ian's making, or probably that girl either.

We're just heading across the bottom of Ian's pasture when a car door slams up by the house. "Hang on," Ian says. He runs toward the blue Ford in the driveway, and somehow I know this is the end of our beach walk.

The motor of the old car starts up. The windshield hides the details of the driver's face, but I can tell it's a girl and she's mad. Ian leans his head in the window. The girl backs off. Ian reaches into the car and wraps a hand around the back of her head. He's kissing her then and the car door opens. Their mouths stay stuck together for ages through the window, even as the girl swings her legs out of the car. How can they do that, and still breathe? I feel like I shouldn't be watching but I can't help it. And they are out in the open, it's not like I'm spying or anything.

Finally they stop kissing long enough for the girl to stand up. Then Ian's got her sandwiched between him and the car. I keep calling her a girl, but she looks about twenty. Ian's pressing against her with his hips and she's pressing back. She doesn't look mad any more. How'd he get her from mad to – to that – so fast? Ian's hands start wandering down the girl's jeans. That's when I hear Dad calling me across the pasture. I start back and Ian calls out, without letting go of the girl, "See you in six weeks."

Right. I knew Ian had girlfriends before, but not like this. I've kissed a girl, once, at a party. And really, she kissed me. Only I didn't know that's what she was going to do, so it kind of missed.

Jill

I can't move. Several cars whiz by the stifling phone booth. Then there's silence.

I can't go to Sheila's, she's not there. I can't go home either. This was supposed to just be a few days away from the tension that's been building between everybody. But now it's broken wide open and it feels like home isn't there to go back to.

What a difference Mark made. He was the most dependable thing about my family. He changed least of anybody when our life out west fell apart. Now he's not even there.

I'll go to Antigonish and find him.

But how can I? I don't have a clue who Amy's aunt is. And they might not even be *in* Antigonish. "*Up near* Antigonish," Charlotte said. God, that could be anywhere.

The thought of going back home without Mark there makes me feel sick to my stomach. I bash open the door of the stuffy phone booth and gulp the fresh air. Only it's hot too. But at least the breeze cools the sweat that's running down my face and sides.

A humungous crow looks down on me from the top of a high tree, disapproving. *You really made a mess of things this time, didn't you?* Same damn judge that was watching me yesterday, I bet.

I grab a large stone from the side of the highway and hurl it, cursing the mangy buzzard. I know I can't hit it, but somehow the *thud* when the stone lands in the gravel makes me feel like anything I try will be absolutely useless. I mean, the stupid thing hasn't even moved.

Another car drones louder, approaching, then away. And silence. I gotta get out of here. But still the question, to where? The not-knowing sits in my stomach like a lump of undigested oatmeal.

Across the highway, there's a luncheonette, the Clam-N-Burger. That'll do for starters.

I slide into an empty booth near the back. The stink of hot fat and burgers hangs in the air. Dishes clatter. Cooks shout. A grumpy-looking waitress swipes a damp cloth over the table, sloshes some water into a glass, and hands me a greasy menu.

This is what my mom does in Halifax. For hours every day.

The waitress loads up her arms with plates from the kitchen and takes them to a group of wiseguys by the window. She starts to put the meals in front of them. Someone says, "This isn't mine." Someone else says, "I didn't order fries." A couple of them laugh like they're the funniest thing since Steve Martin.

Poor Ma. She must put up with this all the time. Not so much at the Swiss Chalet maybe, but that other place she works isn't a whole lot better than this dump.

Finally the pigs by the window have their meals, piles and piles of fries and clams, as if by giving the customers more, the owners think they can make up for how bad the food is.

I used to feel sorry for my mom on account of how hard she works. Partly I still do. But she keeps going along with my dad, no matter how he screws up. So it's hard to have much sympathy.

We should never have left Vancouver. I know we couldn't afford to stay in West Van, but there's lots of cheaper places in the north part of the city. And she could've got a job in one of the good restaurants where you can make tons of money in tips. Without my dad around to gamble it all away, the three of us could've done just fine. I could even have taken the bus and kept going to the same school with all my friends I've known since Grade One. Instead of moving way out here 'cause of some stupid "opportunity" my dad cooked up.

Why did Ma believe him? He's such a liar, and a crook, and I hate him. I'll never go back and live in the same house with him.

So, this is it. No holiday in the country any more, and not what I planned, it's what Chad asked in the Fish House this morning.

I've run away from home.

"Just a milkshake please," I tell the waitress who's come to my table. "Chocolate."

A couple of kids in the booth across from me, about my age, lean across their table at each other, sharing a plate of fries. I try not to stare, but out of the corner of my eye I can see them. The girl takes a long french-fry and dangles it from between her lips. The boy leans closer and nibbles on the end of the fry till they're kissing. Then she eats one from between his lips. It's hard to imagine my parents might've acted like that once. But just last week I caught them in the kitchen in a – what do you call it? – a real hot embrace, let's say. So they probably did.

If only Dad hadn't made such a mess of everything.

But he did. Now Mark's way the hell up near Antigonish, and I'm somewhere between Liverpool and Yarmouth. In other words, in the middle of nowhere.

A little red car like the one I got here in yesterday pulls up outside. It gives me an idea. I can go anywhere now. I can go back to B.C. It would take a lot of rides, but why not? When I get there I can write a letter telling my mom not to worry, I've just "gone home". I wish I could let Mark know somehow. He could come too, and Amy. Too bad.

There's just one problem. Ma called the cops. She knows I've hated living here from the start and how upset I was about Dad and the dance money, on top of everything with Mark, so she must figure I've run away. That means the cops'll be looking for me exactly where I'm heading. Kids who've had it with small eastern towns go west, maybe only to Montreal or Toronto, but it doesn't matter. If I head for Vancouver now, they'll find me, and take me back to Halifax. If I waited a couple of days – they won't bother looking more than that – I'd have a lot better chance.

The waitress plops down my milkshake. Strawberry, but who cares? I sip it down slowly. It's supposed to make you feel fuller if you eat slow, and I can't afford to fill myself up any other way. Thing is, I don't even feel hungry right now. But you can bet if I don't have something now, I'll be starving by the time I get back to that old barn.

Yeah, that's where I'm going. 'Cause no one'll look for me there. And Chad'll help me again. I know he will.

My crow – well okay, maybe it's a different one – is still on duty in the tree. I hoist my knapsack higher on my shoulder and give him the finger. I stop in at the store for a bag of chips and a Coke, in case I get hungry before I can talk to Chad again.

"Hi, honey," says the woman behind the counter, the same one who goofed up about the Merritts and Merrills yesterday. "Find your friend's place okay?"

I tell her I did and head out and down the long gravel road. The mournful tune of that old Beatles song, "She's Leaving Home", plays over and over in my head.

Chad
Our first full day here and they're getting organized for a trip into town. That's why Dad was calling me. He and Gran have done a big shopping list, and Gran has arranged for a late lunch with her sister in Liverpool. We'll also be stopping at Sobey's, Stedman's, Canadian Tire, and if I know Gran, half a dozen other stores as well. None of them reasons I look forward to coming to Dutchman's Bay.

Gramp comes across the field from the quiet Fish House, with more of a spring in his step, I think, than when he headed out. He walks up behind Gran, pulling dry clothes from the line, and kisses her on the back of the neck. She's not the only one surprised. Is he looking forward to this outing, or has his visit to the Fish House had this effect on him?

I could use some time in the Fish House myself. But the day is about to disappear. It'll be late afternoon before we come back from town. If only I didn't have to go, it would be a perfect chance.

"Would it be okay," I suggest, "if I stayed here?"

"Instead of coming with us?" asks Dad, as if this were an extremely radical plan. "I'd rather you came along. I don't like the idea of your being here alone."

"I'm not some little kid, Dad," I insist, "and you don't need me in town." What Ian said — *Parents don't like to give you space unless you make them* — echoes in my head. Finally I come up with an excuse that sounds convincing — "Besides, Ian's going to be working this summer. Today's my last chance to see him."

I've got to Gran with that one. "Gord?"

Dad agrees, with some reluctance. But I can live with that if it gets me another go at my painting.

As soon as they're gone, I grab a peanut butter sandwich to eat on the way down to the Fish House. The hot sun has dried the field and the bushes, but here and there a drop of water glistens on a leaf. I should try painting that, close up. But making water look like water can be hard. A single drop wouldn't be as hard as the sea, because you don't have the movement. But — I'll wait.

It's always cooler in the woods, but near the bend in the path where a tree came down this winter, I feel an unexpected shiver. The chill stays with me, and I need to feel the comfort of the sun's warmth on my skin for a minute, before I turn and go into the Fish House.

With everyone gone into town, I don't really have to hide up here to paint. It'll be hours before they're back. I could take my paints out onto the rocks, along toward Dead Man's, or toward Whaleback. Even over to that great spot in the dunes where Mom and I painted last summer.

But there's something inspiring about being up here too. The way the windows frame different pictures? How the sounds of the sea drift in the open window downstairs? The safe protected feeling here? I don't know, but I like it.

The box of paints is open on the floor, and a fresh sheet of paper inviting me to start. Something new. I clear away this morning's bad starts, and think about beginning again. I screw off the tops of several tubes of paint, smudging a little dab of each on the big shell. With the finest brush I try out a sample of each colour on the edge of the paper. I fold the paper and carefully tear it into four smaller pieces.

A small painting this time. I can see how to compose it. The overturned washtub taking up the lower right section in the foreground, the grass and Queen Anne's lace growing up around it in the middle, with just a thin margin of background sky. It's not quite how it looks from up here, but it would from down beside it. I go down the ladder and outside to have a look.

The light would be better in the morning. This afternoon the shadows aren't right. Not as good as they could be anyway.

I go back into the Fish House and put the ladder back under the maps, ignoring the voice inside me that tells me I'm quitting. Again. That I'm blowing the best chance I'll have this summer.

There's not much point in heading back up to the house or over to Ian's. He'll be busy with the girl in the blue Ford. Or maybe by now he's gone off to his job. And I never even found out where it was, or anything. I might as well go to the beach.

I start along the rocks at the base of the cliff. Waves slosh up through tight spaces in the rocks, pluck-plocking between when the sea surges in and hisses out. Soggy cushions of seaweed cling to the rocks.

I stoop down to look at the grape-like clumps of sea rockets. That's probably not their real name, but it's what I've called them ever since I was little, 'cause that's what they feel like when you bite down on them. Most mothers would probably yell at their kids for putting something like that in their mouths, but Mom's the one who told me to try it.

A couple of years ago she also taught me how to make a frame with my fingers to help pick out part of a scene or an object to draw. I do that now, and close one eye, to focus on one arrangement of the sea rockets, then move on.

I leave my shoes at Whaleback Rock, and wander along the curve of the first beach. Seagulls circle overhead, dip to the water, and fly off with their finds.

I wade across Tickle Creek, the rusty trickle of fresh water that runs out of Black Lake, then meander around the last rocky piece of shoreline. The long sandy beach stretches out in front of me. The dunes rise gradually along the back of the beach, all the way over to the Nile River, which you can't see from here, but it's just before the next point of land jutting out into the sea – Picnic Point we call it. You wouldn't find the Nile on any Nova Scotia map. It's really small, and it changes direction from year to year, week to week sometimes, down at the beach end anyway. The Nile River is the name my mom gave it because when I was about knee-high to a grasshopper I said it was like crossing the desert to get there.

The sun is hot, right overhead, but for an instant I feel the same peculiar shiver I felt back in the woods. Then I see why. There's a mist, very fine, rolling in from the sea. Gees, it's weird how the weather around here can change from one moment to the next.

The mist is swirling in strange shapes. It often does down here before it closes in the bay completely. But this is different. I blink, trying to make sense of what I'm seeing.

Gradually, near where I'm standing, the mist becomes less — I don't know — misty. There's colour in it, the shapes it's swirling in more defined. Like a woman. The sea is lapping at her ankles and the edge of her long skirt. One hand is resting on her hip, the other is reaching — toward me? No, she's at an easel. The woman turns her head and I see her face. What has appeared, not twenty feet away, is my mother.

I step toward her, elated. I must take five or six fumbling steps — and almost touch her — before she, the mist, turns and whispers something that gets lost in the *shwish* of a wave, and disappears. I fall to my knees at the water's edge. The waves wash away the last traces of her, the impressions of her feet in the wet sand.

I want her back. I sob shamelessly with how much. I curl forward onto my elbows. The sea washes up my bare arms and soaks into my jeans. Nothing will ever heal the huge emptiness in me. I grab handfuls of wet sand, hard and gritty, that the sea pulls away, empties. I get up then and storm to the place in the dunes where last year we painted. As if somehow this will bring her back. If only in the way she was here a minute ago.

The dune grass tickles at my feet, but there's no trace of her there. Or at the water's edge where I'm pulled again. I trudge back up the beach toward the dunes.

But no. She's gone. Of course, I knew that before. I have known it for months. But not like I know it now.

I drop to the warm sand at the base of the dunes and again, as I lie there, the tears come. Then the strangest image comes into my head — I've crawled into my father's lap and I'm curled up there, sucking my thumb.

Jill

It's funny how much like home the old barn feels when I climb the stairs to my loft, hot and sweaty. There's no birds to welcome me this time. I take off my sweatshirt, hang it on a rusty nail, and pull on the first cooler thing I come to in my knapsack, a black T-shirt. I consider unpacking the rest of my things, but think better of it. When you're somewhere you don't belong, you never know when you might have to leave in a hurry.

I look out my cracked window. People out west pay a bundle for a sea-view like this. And here I am enjoying it for free — the bobbing heads of wild carrot in the field below me almost as far as the path, then bushes and small trees over the hills that drop to the sea, the beach that curves around the bay. I feel good, like my plan to stay here's going to work.

There's no sign of Chad or anyone. They've probably gone to the beach. It's a gorgeous afternoon.

I'd love to be down there. If I knew for sure that's where Chad's family is, I could raid the kitchen for a few things.

But I'd better wait for him. Trekking to the beach is probably more than his grandparents are capable of. They might be right in the kitchen having a cup of tea or something.

Standing at the window, I think about Chad's family, everyone getting along and spending time with each other. I imagine I'm actually part of it. Only I'm a secret part. I'm the crazy relation they have to keep hidden. Don't laugh. Families used to do that with relatives who had things wrong with them they didn't understand, like if they were mentally retarded, or stuff like that that might bring shame to their family name.

Naturally my family loves me too much to put me in an institution, so they keep me at home in the attic. When they go on holidays they hide me under a blanket on the floor of the car, and then in their barn when they get here. Because the attic of their house here is used for something else. The family jewels. Or my brother's bedroom perhaps. The prince.

Too bad they didn't give me the car blanket up here. It would beat sleeping on the bare straw. One of them will probably bring it later. Chad. When he brings me my dinner on the Merrill silver platter.

He will help me for a couple of days, won't he? — before I head out to B.C.?

I've been standing at the window for a while before it clicks. One of the cars is gone. Who's gone? All of them?

I still can't go to the house. Anybody could answer the door, and how would I explain? But I can't stay in the barn forever. Chad's not going to come again till he knows I'm back. Eventually I'll have to go out to find him. Could he be at the beach? Or at the Fish House? Do other people really use that building, or was he just trying to keep me out of there?

The beach is probably my best bet. If I do bump into someone besides Chad, I can just nod and say hello. They won't know if I'm visiting around here or what. I'll take the back route to the Fish House and then, if Chad's not there, go along the rocks to the beach.

Now that I know I'm never going home and that the cops are probably looking for me, it matters, more than this morning, that nobody finds me here. That'd be great, eh? — to blow my perfect hiding place 'cause I got caught up on some stupid trespassing charge? But once decided, I'm quickly on my way, careful but keyed up.

The rhythm of the sea washing up around the Fish House calms me down. There's no window in the back, so to look in I'll have to creep around to the sea side. But if anyone's in there, that's where they'll be looking.

Better to risk opening the door a crack and peeking in than to go for the front window.

I'd forgotten there was a window in the door, small and high up.

I tiptoe on the step. The room's empty. There's no one there. I look in again. The ladder's against the wall, so Chad's not upstairs either.

The Fish House is so inviting, right on the sea and everything. I could be happy here forever. It's cleaner than the barn, and I wouldn't have to share it with a bunch of stupid swallows. I'm tempted just to move my things here from the barn, but Chad was so dead set against that this morning, and even here I'd need his help. I'll wait and try out the idea again when I find him.

The water and sky are a deep and brilliant blue. It's a magnificent shoreline, if you like rocks, and I do. I almost skip from one to another, feeling safe and secure with the cliff on one side of me and the sea lapping up on the other.

I hear a strange barking sound, and slow down. It's quiet, the only sound the relaxed movement of the sea. I squint toward the animal noise.

It's two seals. Just for a moment I see their heads – unless it's just rocks below the surface – then they're gone. When they appear next they're closer, definitely seals. I stare, entranced, as they dive and swim about. For a brief moment I'm tempted to join them, like someone in a kid's book might do.

The seals could be my family. We'd swim and dive and have all kinds of wonderful adventures together all day, and at night I'd go into the warm Fish House while my seals rest on the rocks outside my window. Do seals sleep at night?

They've taken a break from their playing. And spotted me here on the rocks. They're staring. Just as I've been staring at them. I turn away, and continue along the rocks self-consciously. "Go swim."

I've come a long way by the time I lose them, to a huge rock. There's no sheltering cliff beside me any more. Instead there's a grassy meadow with woods behind it. The shoreline becomes sandy beach here, with just one section of rock between here and the point across the bay.

Beside the huge rock is one pair of shoes, a kind of beat-up pair of runners. Is Chad alone down here then? I can't see anyone along the whole stretch of sandy beach, but he can't be too far away.

I don't dare leave my shoes out in the open, but I lean against the huge rock to take them off and tie them to one of the belt-loops on my jeans. I roll up the legs of my jeans, and step into the water. The hard ripples of sand under my feet and the cool water lapping against my shins is sheer heaven.

But I better make the most of this chance to find Chad. If I get sidetracked like I did yesterday – was that really only yesterday? – I could end up starving in that stupid barn again tomorrow morning. I move to shallower water and head more determined along the beach.

I've just passed a little creek and a tumble of rocks when I see him. He's alone, but suddenly I'm afraid. He could turn me away. Just 'cause he brought me something once doesn't mean he'll do it again, especially if I need him for a few days.

I move slowly closer. It looks like he's asleep. There's almost six feet of him stretched out there but for some reason he reminds me of a little boy. Except I can imagine being stretched out beside him, and not in the way I've stretched out with the two-year-old I babysit who needs me there to help him go to sleep sometimes. No, if I was lying beside Chad, he'd have his arms around me, and — he opens his eyes then. He's surprised to see me, more than I expected. No, I guess what's unexpected is his smile.

Chad

Something casts a shadow across my face. My heart beats fast. I can't say what I was expecting when I open my eyes, but it's not the girl from the barn. She sits down, and digs her feet into the sand. I know without her saying so that she needs me to help her again.

The sun is shining down and the breeze is blowing across the sand, harder than — well — harder than before. I imagine she's trying to figure out how to get me to do something for her, without having to tell me why.

"I need to stay for a few days," she says.

I shrug and tell her, "'Kay."

The waves push in to shore, getting stronger and louder as they merge with each other, and finally crashing, send a wash that shines high up onto the beach. Then they whisper away. This girl seems as free to me as the sandpipers skittering over the mirror at the water's edge.

If I had her kind of guts, I know, I wouldn't be in the bind I am with my father. I probably wouldn't run away like she's done, but somehow I'd be able to say, "This isn't what I want."

I tell her I forget her name and she tells me. "I'm Chad," I say.

She laughs and says, "I remember." It's hard to take my eyes off her face when she smiles. It comes and goes so quickly. I wish I knew how to make it happen again.

"Look at the sandpipers," I say.

She smiles again. "They look like they're running on tiptoe, don't they."

No one suggests it but soon we're walking along the beach, above the high-tide line where the sea has tossed bits of seaweed, now dry and crinkly. Warm sand hugs the soles of our feet.

Once, our hands brush against each other. I shove mine into my pockets so they don't flap around so much.

Farther on I stop to study some patterns the retreating tide has etched in the sand, guided by sprawling bits of tangled seaweed. I can imagine sitting for hours trying to capture the intricate twistings and turnings on paper, working just with a sharp pencil or, with watercolour, imitating the curving branches in the sand that flow toward the shining flats, shrinking gradually with the rising tide. If I were going to paint again, that is.

"They're beautiful, aren't they," Jill says.

I nod at her and smile.

"They make pictures," she says. "Look, here's a troll with a long nose and a beard. And look at this one."

Four separate strands extend from a long slender body. They're like the arms and legs of a dancer.

It must be how she saw them too. Because she's off, like the pattern come to life on the beach, leaping into the air, her arms stretched above her head, then twirling, whirling, and leaping again. Then her rhythm changes, as if she's hearing a different music in her head. She kicks and spins and stretches and twists, dancing in the wide open space by the sea. What does she hear? Vanilla Ice? Pat Metheny? Or the "Hallelujah Chorus"?

It's fabulous what she's doing, like she's forgotten where she is, like there's some force inside her giving energy to her movement. The way it used to feel for me when my painting was going well. Seagull on air. Air on water. Water on rock. The music of the sea filling my head, like it's filling hers now.

She finishes on her knees, leaning back. Her hair hangs behind her to the sand.

"Nice," I say when she's rearranged herself so she's sitting cross-legged. "Are you a dancer?" Dumb question. But her answer surprises me.

Shaking her tangled mane of hair, she says, "Not any more."

"Why not?"

Her eyes cloud over. "You," she says as if I was some miserable disease, "wouldn't understand."

A minute ago I was wondering if I might talk to her about the painting I used to do, but in a matter of seconds she's turned back into that sullen quick-tempered I-don't-know-what who showed up at the Fish House yesterday. No, not yesterday, that was just this morning.

What's the story behind this mysterious stranger who has appeared in my life out of nowhere?

As if she read my thoughts, Jill says, "My dad stole the money my mom put aside for my classes and lost it on a horse race." I don't know what to say, but she goes on. "She'll never earn enough to keep up with how fast he can gamble it away."

"That's kind of like a disease, isn't it?" I say. "Like being alcoholic, only you're addicted to gambling instead?"

"I don't know."

"They've got groups for it I think."

"I don't care what his problem is. I'm not going back there."

"What about your mom?"

"She's no hell either. I mean, she works her butt off to support this oaf, 'cause she's too chicken to make him pull his own weight, or else ditch him."

"Maybe you're lucky to have her," I say.

"Aahh, what's the matter, Chad?" she sneers. "Is your mommy gone away? Did your parents get a divorce?" She gets up and bashes the sand off her jeans. Her tone hardens. "I wish my parents would get a divorce. But my mother's too stupid to know when she's better off . . . "

"She's dead."

Jill has started down the beach but stops. I half expect her to storm off and say she wishes *her* mom was, but she doesn't. She just stands there with her back to me. Her defiant shoulders have dropped. Her head too, and all her muscles seem collapsed, like a marionette whose strings got suddenly loosened. The wind is whipping at her hair and loose T-shirt. Otherwise she's perfectly still.

I blurt it all out. About the football game and the rain. The truck on the curve. The cop showing up at the stadium with my dad. How my aunts and uncles stared at me at the funeral and told me after it was okay to cry and I shouldn't hold it in, only I wasn't holding anything in, there wasn't anything to hold in then. I tell her what a good painter she was and how I blame myself for the accident because I could have just taken a bus. And how my dad must blame me too, and how it might be easier if he would. I tell her a whole bunch of things I didn't even know I knew, and somewhere in there she comes over and sits down again beside me. I almost tell her about what I saw on the beach, back toward Tickle Creek and the rocks, but suddenly I feel dumb for having already said what I have. So I stop.

Jill doesn't say "I'm sorry" like most people would, and she doesn't apologize for being so awful either, or say something fake about her own mother and how she should appreciate her. I'm surprised I've blurted out so much to her and I'm surprised at how sensitive she is. I thought she was so tough. She points to Picnic Point. "Can we walk out there?"

We continue along the beach. She's still not saying much, just looking out to sea, or commenting on the odd shell she finds. I'm feeling lighter somehow. I'd like to take her hand and walk with her together. But just because she let me talk about all that stuff without thinking it was dumb doesn't mean she likes me like that. Maybe when we get to the Nile.

Just then she sprints ahead. She turns and calls back to me, "Run."

I holler, "Why are we running?"

The wind carries her answer, "Because I feel like it."

I race to catch up with her. At the stream she splashes across, soaking the bottoms of her jeans where they're rolled just below her knees. I charge across after her, taking a long leap across the narrowest part so only one leg of my jeans gets soaked.

We start out along Picnic Point, slowly now, because of the rocks. Without shoes, some of them are quite rough, even sharp. There's a flat grassy part up from the rocks that's good for picnics — that's how the place got its name — but since neither of us brought lunch, we decide to head back to the beach.

Behind me, Jill says, "Come look at the colours in here."

I work my way down to where she's crouching beside a tidal pool in the top of a wrinkled-looking rock. Below the clear water, purple mussels are clinging to pink rock. Chunks of white quartz jut here and there through the pink. Delicate tendrils of plants in shades of turquoise, magenta, and green flutter in the pool.

"Did your mother paint things like this?" Jill asks. She's still staring into the tidal pool teeming with life.

"Yeah." I can't get the words out to say it's the kind of thing she liked painting best.

A single tear drops into the pool, ripples its stillness. "It's beautiful, isn't it," Jill whispers. She looks up at me with wet eyes, bites her lower lip, and tries to smile. "I love it here."

"Me too." I'm glad she came back, but I don't tell her.

When we're back at the mouth of the stream, with the soft sand underfoot again, Jill points across the bay. "That's your house up on the hill, isn't it? And the barn?"

"Yeah."

"Oh, you can see the Fish House from here too."

The fields and the buildings and the rocks and the woods make a hilly country seaside scene, like English teachers make you write poems about. This is a vantage point I don't think my mother ever used for a painting. I mentally block it out on my page — where the horizon line would go, how much space to give the shoreline, the rough placement of the buildings.

"I really would love to stay down there instead of in the barn," Jill says.

I haven't been as awful to her as I was this morning, so I can't exactly blame her for asking again. But I'm all confused. I think I'm giving up as a painter, but then can't stop seeing things that way. Jill could be a real bother there, but. . . .

"Never mind," she says.

"I'm just not sure . . ."

"No, it's okay," she insists. "I'm lucky you're willing to help me out."

"We should maybe go back and get some food for you to take to the barn while everybody's still away."

"There's just one thing I want to do first," she says brightly. "More than anything."

"What's that?"

"I want to swim in the ocean," she says. "Don't look."

And before I can look away or say anything, she slips her black T-shirt over her head – her bare breasts are right there, creamy and smooth – and pulls off her jeans. She's totally naked and I look away then. But the only naked female I've ever seen was in a magazine of Ian's. I can't not look.

She runs fast into the water. Throwing herself into the waves she lets out a shriek. She bobs underwater, kicks, and splashes. From time to time skin that's never seen the sun breaks the surface.

Then only her face and her dark hair plastered to the sides of her head are above the water. "It's cold," she shouts. "I have to get out now."

She's going to come up here. I should be doing something. She's as good as invited me, hasn't she? What would Ian do? Run his hands all over her, and kiss her, and lower her to the sand. I can picture it all in my mind. I just can't see myself doing it.

I fix my eyes on a tree in back of the dunes, and walk hard along the beach. I turn back once, and catch a glimpse of her rising from the sea, the mass of hair dripping round her face, her lovely jiggling breasts, the dark tuft of hair beneath her belly.

I stop at the spill of rocks next to Tickle Creek and plunk myself down. The water is gurgling and splashing up between them and over them. A ridge of clouds is moving in over Dead Man's Point.

"That feels better," Jill says.

For you maybe.

"I don't remember crossing these rocks before," she says.

"Tide's come in."

"Oh, right."

"It would be hard to get around them now, unless you want to go for another swim." I'm only partly kidding. Some other part is mad, probably as much at myself for not knowing how to handle it as at her for making me feel so dumb.

She goes all quiet then, running her toe in circles in the sand. "I feel kind of silly about that now," she says. "I don't make a habit of throwing off my clothes in front of guys, you know."

"Well, I felt kind of dumb 'cause I never had a girl do that before. I wasn't sure if I was supposed to — you know — do something."

"I'm sorry."

I shove the hair off my face. I admit to her, "Just looking felt like doing."

"You're nice, Chad." Her dark hair drips into her black T-shirt. Her eyes smile at me. I want to say something "nice". I want to tell her she's beautiful.

"Your lips," I say, "are blue."

She bites them. They're still a bit blue, and moist. "Is that better?"

Another invitation. But instead of just leaning over and doing it — kissing her — I hear myself saying, "Let's get back."

I know, I sound like a real chicken. But the sun's getting lower in the sky, and if we're going to stop at the house, it's true, we should get back.

We cross the rocks as quickly as we can in bare feet, and start around the curve of the smaller beach between Tickle Creek and Whaleback Rock. But it's hard to hurry Jill when she doesn't feel like hurrying. It's as if being down on the beach has made her forget everything, the fact that she doesn't want anyone to know she's here, and even whatever it is that brought her here.

We're almost to Whaleback when she stops. "Look, Chad."

In her hand lies a perfect sand dollar, white and unchipped. I'd like to say something about it helping her remember me when she leaves here, or about it standing for the afternoon, but the words sound dumb in my head. They'd sound even dumber if I tried to say them.

"Did you know," Jill asks, "that inside a sand dollar there are five birds?"

"No."

"They're supposed to represent the doves of peace."

I nod. "If we don't get going. . . . "

She slips the sand dollar carefully into her jeans pocket. I guess she finally starts to share my sense of urgency then because she pulls on her shoes at Whaleback when I do, and makes no more stops, wet or otherwise, before we get back to the house.

Jill

Chad assures me his grandmother'll throw this stuff out to make room for the new groceries anyway – a leftover chicken leg out of the back of the fridge, a bruised apple, the tail end of a box of crackers, one of those little juice boxes, the last of a chunk of cheddar, the remains of a jar of applesauce, and a rather wizened looking baked potato. He chucks it all in a bag, then quickly, I go back to the barn.

Right away I'm at the window.

I love being by the sea. And it felt so safe down on the beach. Maybe 'cause that kind of place is linked in my mind to the happy parts of when I was little. But there was something different about Chad this afternoon, too. It might have something to do with the beach, I don't know. Near the end he was getting real antsy to get me back to the barn, but it wasn't like he resented me being around like this morning. In a way he seemed happy to have me there.

He's sure not used to girls though. But I guess it didn't help having me prancing around in my birthday suit. Poor guy didn't know where to look.

I kind of liked him looking though. But that's not why I did it. I just felt so grungy from sleeping in the barn and all that dusty walking, I had to get in the water. I couldn't go in dressed 'cause the sky was hazing over and without the sun I would've been too cold in my wet clothes, after. Besides, me and Charlotte and Mark and a couple of his friends — we've skinny-dipped before, at night at that little beach just outside the city. It was no big deal really. But today it was suddenly — well — different. It embarrassed Chad too. That made me almost sorry I did it.

I bite into the apple Chad gave me. It's early for a meal, but I didn't have much of a lunch. I decide to save the rest of the apple for after I've eaten everything else, since even though I've got my toothbrush, I don't relish the idea of brushing my teeth with orange juice. I wolf down the chicken leg, then open the applesauce. I don't have a spoon, so I tip the jar up and pour the sweet mush bit by bit into my mouth. I run my finger around the inside of the jar, and lick and suck it till the fruity taste is gone.

It's not right that all this would've got thrown out, but I guess in my situation I should be grateful. My mom always uses up leftovers, and did when we lived in Vancouver too, before we had to worry about the cost of everything. It's weird how I feel drawn to Chad somehow, at the same time it chafes me how much he's got. Maybe I'm just a sucker for him 'cause of how he opened up to me about his mother getting killed and everything. Other guys I know would never do that. It wasn't easy for him either, I could tell. But I guess, like Mark says, I'm a good listener.

Chad reminds me a bit of Mark in some ways. That probably sounds stupid, seeing how Mark has a pregnant girlfriend and Chad was too scared to even kiss me. But Mark was real shy about girls too for a while, and even lately he never bragged about making it with Amy or anything. Also, there's something about the way Chad holds his chin when he's mad that reminds me of Mark too.

I feel tears coming on me. I'm not usually such a cry-baby, but thinking of Mark I can't help it. Will I ever see him again? I reach into my pocket for a kleenex. My fingers touch the sand dollar I found this afternoon. I hope it's not broken. No. I hold it between my palms like a good luck talisman.

I open my hand and run a finger over the design in the top of it. That's supposed to stand for something too, like the tiny chips of shell inside are supposed to be doves of peace. Can a person get reincarnated as a sand dollar, and then become the flower, or star, or dancer — whatever the design on top might be?

I could be a star with my very own space, guiding shepherds. No, forget the shepherds. I could be a flower cheering up a lonely table, or be part of a garden by a stone cottage. Or I could be a dancer, spinning and floating, caring for nothing but the circle I dance, the circle of the perfect sun-bleached disk.

Better still I could be the sand dollar itself, lying on the beach, warmed by the sun, surrounded by the forever sea sounds. Till Chad comes along and finds me, holds me gently in his hand.

Why does everything have to come back to *him*?

I slip the sand dollar back into my pocket, out of sight. But I can't get Chad out of my mind that easily. He's been sweet, even if he doesn't want me at his Fish House. He's gone back there, I think. I watched him crossing the field. And who am I to him but some stupid chick begging for his help? Does he know that's not what I'm like? That in real life I'm strong and independent? I should tell him I'm going to B.C. to get away from the mess I've left behind and to start my own life.

But what's it matter? As long as he keeps bringing me food, what does it matter what he thinks?

Chad

Safely back at the barn, Jill waves to me and disappears. Tall shadows stretch across the field. A barn swallow swoops out the broken window.

I could do that too, soar and float and swoop over the hills and sea. I leap down the steps, my heart racing. I've got to go to the Fish House. Not to *try* to paint this time. I *know* I can.

I hurry through the cool woods, almost skip down the mossy downslope toward the sea, then scamper over the rocks.

The oak box lies on the floor at my feet with parts of its rainbow missing. The rest of the tubes are on the windowsill. The colour moves from my palette to my brush to my paper as if I'm pulling the pigments right out of the sky and sea, capturing every tone from nature for my own. Veridian Lake. Prussian Blue. Payne's Grey. Indigo. Alizarin Rose Madder. Ultramarine.

Soon the colours on the palette, on the paper, outside the window, the sea breeze washing in with the rush of the waves, are all that exist. Lines and lines and lines flow onto the page. Curving, Jill cuts through the waves and waves wash over Jill. The water tones and skin tones reflect off each other. Jill's curves merge with the curves of the sea. The waves dance in response to her being among them. It's not clear where the sea and the woman begin, where the woman and the sea end.

With some rusty tacks I find in an old bucket, I hang the painting on the wall and sit down to begin another. Part of me I didn't know was there has taken over. Outside, a light mist has rolled in, changing the landscape again.

"Changes ..." I tap the end of my paintbrush against the windowsill in time to the stuttery music. "Changes. . . ." It's what I've always loved about the sea. But I've always felt so insignificant in the face of its power. Until today. If I can do what I'm doing here, then I've got some of that power too, from that mermaid holing up in my grandparents' Old Barn.

I do four more paintings before I remember I ought to get back to the house. Dad especially will be wondering where I am. Beside the one of Jill-in-the-sea-in-Jill, I tack up the others – the old pine growing in the rocks over by Whaleback, the thistle in the floor of the Old Barn, the Old Barn itself. And my favourite one, except for Jill's, the mist rising from the sea in the shape of my mother.

As I push the last tack into its top corner, I know what the whispered word was that I didn't hear down by the dunes this afternoon. Painter.

Jill

Rain's pattering against the barn. The birds in the rafters are quiet company. Chad's family came back a while ago. I heard the car, and watched them unpack. Chad came back, from the Fish House probably, not long after. What's he do there?

Drizzly dusk is settling over the hills and fields. I pull on a sweatshirt, saving my jacket for later, when I'm going to sleep. I should've asked Chad about a blanket when we were in the house. Will he be able to get out here tonight, or will I have to wait till tomorrow? I should probably stay here another night after this one, maybe two, before I head out west.

It's funny. It's not just liking where I am that makes me feel sort of scared about going all that way on my own. It's being near Chad, or his family, or something. I don't know. I shouldn't probably think about it too much. It's just this drizzle's got me feeling a little low.

There's a sound outside, familiar, but not one of the sea sounds. I look out my knothole. Pulling up beside the house is an RCMP cruiser. Two cops step out of the blue and white car, take a quick look around, and slam their doors. They climb the side steps I watched Chad working on this morning, before I went out to the highway and found out my life was even more upside down than I thought.

And it just got worse.

What will Chad do? Will he think I'm some kind of a crook, or druggie, or something? He's such a straight and narrow guy. That's part of what I like about him in some weird way, but will he be able to keep his mouth shut if a Mountie asks him point blank, *Have you seen this girl?*

They could be here about something else — the vandalism to that other house maybe, or someone stealing sheep.

But I can't take any chances. I make sure everything's stuffed in my knapsack and tear out of there.

Chad

I'm chopping vegetables for supper with Gran when there's a knock at the door. I've been feeling pleased about the bag I put together for Jill when I was "helping put the groceries away", so for the briefest instant I think it's her at the door. Not really, but I'm surprised when two police officers step into the kitchen.

At first I don't connect them with Jill. Not till one of them drops the photographs on the table. "We have a teenaged Halifax girl reported missing and reason to believe she might be in the area."

And it's Jill all right. No question of that.

The photos are a strip of black and white shots taken in one of those booths like they've got in train stations. Were these the best her family had? In two of them she's clowning around with some guy who's got his arm around her — I can't believe at a time like this I'm actually capable of feeling jealous.

Whoever this guy is, her eyes in one of the serious shots are looking up at me, like they did from the bottom of the ladder in the Fish House, and by the tidal pool down on the beach. They're counting on me.

Dad shakes his head. "Sorry," he says, "I haven't seen her."

Gramp says, "We don't get many people down this way."

One of the officers says, "I wouldn't think so, but her parents think she headed in this general direction yesterday and a local merchant says this girl might have been in her store yesterday and again today."

Gran says, "I'm not sure, but I may have seen her."

Everyone stares at her while she thinks. Including me, who wants to tell her, "No, it's okay Gran, you don't have to try and help *everybody*." They'll never give up searching this area if Gran decides she's seen her.

"She's a little like one of the girls on that soap you watch after lunch," says Gramp. "That's all."

Gran fusses with her dish towel. "Yes, perhaps."

I wonder how Gramp knows so much about Gran's soaps.

"That your barn on the hill?" one of the police asks. Somebody must have nodded 'cause he goes on, "Alright with you folks if we check it out?"

"Certainly," Dad says.

Jill

Sounds like the bird's doing a suicide number against the window as I boot it out of there. It's getting dark, but the short space between the barn and the shelter of the woods feels very far. If they come out of the house now they'll see me. I feel so slow and clumsy pushing through the bay bushes. Maybe I'd have been smarter to stay where I was.

Even in the woods the cops feel too close. So I run. I stumble over tree roots and scratch my face on dead branches. I run till the call of the sea rises and I scramble onto the rocks.

I close the door of the Fish House tight behind me. I lean on it, my heart pounding, and catch my breath. This morning when I was here feels like days and not just hours ago.

I lean Chad's ladder into the hole in the ceiling. Halfway up I hoist my knapsack into his room. The ladder jiggles and creaks. I pull it up into the room behind me.

Chad

Waiting for the police to come back from the barn is torture. Will they bring Jill back here? Or just chuck her into the cruiser? I hope she knows I didn't give her away. But what difference does it make? If she's caught, they'll take her home.

Trying to be casual about it, I glance out the window of the side door. There's no sign of anyone between here and the barn. What's happening out there? I crush some garlic and mash it into a dish of butter to keep myself from looking concerned or from ripping Jill's photos from Gran's hand.

A minute that feels like an hour later the cops are back.

"There are signs that someone was there," one of them says, "but whoever it was appears to be gone."

"The girl?" Dad asks.

"We don't know."

I feel the police officer's eyes on me. Suspicious. I slather garlic butter on another hunk of bread. She can't be gone. She knew I was coming back. Unless she left when these guys showed up. But then she won't have gone far.

Trying to sound helpful and hoping like crazy I'm not leading them in the direction she's gone I say, "There's an old abandoned house at the end of this point of land. You'd need a four-wheel drive to get in to it, but someone running away might go somewhere like that."

"We'll check it out. In the meantime, keep this copy of the photos. If you see the girl, or have any other information for us, please give us a call."

Gran closes the door behind them. She clutches the strip of pictures and shakes her head. "I've seen her somewhere, I'm sure of it."

Jill

Except for a piece of driftwood by the far window, where a bit of daylight's still coming in, the upstairs is empty. I cross the rotting floor to a shadowy corner and lie down against my knapsack. If they look up, they're not going to notice through the cracks in the floorboards the dark unmoving shape in the corner, and with no ladder they're not likely to think anyone's up here anyway. I think I'm feeling safe till I realize I'm squeezing my eyes shut, like a kid who thinks, if I can't see you, you can't see me.

I breathe in the salty air, listening for sounds that don't belong, heavy steps or voices, 'cause there's no way of getting a car down here. I lie there long enough to feel sure they're not coming. I open my eyes and feel a bit smug – I got my room in the Fish House after all.

Then I notice the pictures on the wall, curling at the edges, fluttering damply in a shifting breeze. I stand up to get a closer look. I touch my fingers lightly to a painting of the barn where I've been hiding, as if it might be the same rough texture as the barn itself. There are others, of a tree, a thistle, and one of a washed out misty sort of painter standing where the sea meets the sand. And – this one's a bit abstract, but it gives me a definite feeling of being in the water again. In the corner of each painting are the initials, strong and sure, CM.

That he paints doesn't come as a surprise to me. What does is how good he is.

But why's he hiding up here to do it? Is his father, who seems so considerate and loving, some macho pig who doesn't approve?

I sit down on the driftwood by the window as night enters Dutchman's Bay. I imagine Chad working here, loving to paint the way I love to dance. Outside the window the surf rolls in to shore. A rising offshore wind skims the tops off the breaking waves. The rumbling in the surf of small smooth rocks shudders along the shoreline.

In the distance an owl hoots.

Chad

"Chad." Sharp. Like he's annoyed.

"What?" I push my uneaten salad to the side of my plate.

"I've spoken to you twice," Dad says.

"Sorry," I mumble. "What did you say?"

"I asked," – he's obviously trying to sound patient – "what you did with yourself today."

"Oh, um . . ." *I fell in love. I watched a beautiful girl swim naked in the ocean. Then I went to the Fish House and did some of the best painting I've ever done.*

Gramp clears his throat, nudges my knee under the table.

I look up from my plate. Dad's staring at me.

I paste on a smile. "I went for a walk on the beach."

"Is that all?" Dad presses. "We were gone for a long time."

"I went pretty far," I say, "and walked along the rocks too." Nightfall has painted a grey curtain over the kitchen windows and still there hasn't been a decent chance to find out if Jill has come back to the barn. I place my knife and fork across my plate. "May I be excused?"

Gran collects the plates and carries them to the sink. "I was hoping we might play Making Words and Taking Words again tonight."

"Aren't you guys tired," I suggest, "after your big day in town?"

"Whuh?" says Gramp.

"I thought you might be tired."

"We're not too tired for a game," says Gran, as if such an idea were unheard of. She seems disappointed that I'm not more interested, so I try to sound pleased about going to fetch the tiles.

Turning them face down on the table I can't help but notice the growing blackness outside. Every time a letter is turned over I try to make a word. "Oris . . . Thrish." Anything to get the game over with.

"Shirt," Gran pipes up.

"Shirt," I repeat.

"Yes," says Dad, "but I think Gran said it first."

"I left my sweatshirt down on the rocks this afternoon." I push myself away from the table.

"It's dark now, dear," fusses Gran, "why don't you leave it till morning?"

"It's okay," I insist, "I know right where it is."

"I'll come with you." Dad stands up.

"No, Dad. This game's no good with just two people, and you've already got some words. I'm not really in this anyway." I get out of the kitchen fast and take the stairs two at a time, hardly believing I stood up to him.

Quickly I brush my teeth. I pull the other stuff for Jill from under my bed, and roll up everything together in a blanket, including a sweatshirt for me to "find" while I'm out. I push the bundle out the window and knock over my doorstop to cover any sound it might make landing. I run my hands through my hair and grab a flashlight.

"Chad, what were you doing upstairs?"

"Getting my flashlight."

"Is that what fell?"

"No, I accidentally kicked over my doorstop."

"Oh. Chad?" What, what, what? "Did I hear you —
brushing your teeth?"

"Um. Yeah."

"To go find your sweatshirt?"

"It'll save the crush in the bathroom at bedtime."
I shove out into the dark before I can say some other
dumb thing.

Zooks is sniffing the blanket at the side of the
house. "Go home, Zooks," I whisper. He looks up at
me, wagging his tail. "No." I grab the bundle and stamp
my foot. "Go home."

Hoo-hoo-hoooo.

Rocks jut through the uneven ground. Porcupines
in the tall grass and bay bushes flee to escape as I
charge through their night territory. The smell of bay
is strong in the evening damp.

Will she be in the barn? Or will she have disappeared from Dutchman's Bay as mysteriously as she
arrived?

I feel my way along the wall to the stairs. As I
climb, my eyes adjust to the darkness. She's not in the
loft. My insides do a little flip — I didn't really believe
she wouldn't be here. I flick my flashlight on briefly,
just long enough to see that only the panicked birds
are huddled in the barn's dark shadows.

She must have cleared out when the cops came,
but she wouldn't stay hiding in the woods this long.

And heading anywhere else would be way riskier than coming back here, where they've already looked for her.

Anywhere else but where she's wanted to be all along. Anywhere else but the Fish House.

Jill

I'm getting sleepy, but it might be better if Chad doesn't find me in his private space in the morning. I'll tell him I was here, to hide better. It's not that I'd lie to him or anything, But I'll go downstairs in case he shows up early again to do some more painting.

The cops are for sure gone by now. Chad did say people sometimes use the Fish House, but I doubt anyone will be coming down tonight, or before him in the morning. Especially not with the storm that's blowing up.

It hasn't started raining again yet, but the wind's coming up strong. The waves are really roaring out there.

I lower the ladder through the opening in the floor, climb down, and put the ladder back against the wall. The window facing the sea lets a lot more light in down here than the small ones upstairs. Except when the moon slips behind a cloud. The sky changes so quickly that the room's bright with moonlight one moment, then plunged into darkness the next. It's sort of eerie, but I shiver with the excitement of being so near the sea as it revs up for a big storm.

Turning from the window I knock against an old fish box. I lift off the wooden top, not really expecting there to be anything inside. It's just what you do with a box, eh? If I sound a bit defensive, it's 'cause the box isn't empty.

There's a rock in it, about the size and shape of a large potato, sitting on top of a notebook. I pick up the rock and run my finger along a sharp vein of quartz running through it. I wrap my hand around it and squeeze. The room gets dark suddenly — a cloud's blocking the moon. I'm about to put the rock back when the room gets brighter again, and I see on the notebook, in fine calligraphy, "Rocks and Dune Grass: Diary of An Old Man".

I lift the notebook from the box. In the moonlight I make out "by P. G. Merrill" in smaller letters. Pages and pages are filled with his fine printing. Chad's grandfather, a writer.

Suddenly I feel like the intruder that I am. I set the notebook and rock back in the box and shut the lid.

I yank my jacket out of my knapsack, which I then arrange as a pillow in the corner. A denim jacket doesn't make much of a blanket and I shiver at the wet windy sounds of the rising storm.

But the hypnotic rhythms of the sea, so close, rock me, as if I'm cast adrift, but safe, and very soon, I am asleep.

Chad

On the steps of the Fish House I take a second to catch my breath, run a hand through my hair, then I go inside.

The ladder's where I left it, against the wall. And she's not here. Only shadows cast by the bright moonlight. I can't breathe for at least a minute.

But in the dark corner between the door and the front window the moon briefly catches a curve of cheek, then fades. I close my eyes, let out a deep breath.

She's curled up under her jacket, her head resting on her knapsack. Kneeling on the floor beside her I lean close enough to see the darkness of her eyelashes against her pale skin and the dark opening of her mouth. So softly she breathes. My heart's pounding so hard I'm sure the sound will wake her. I lean closer, feel the warmth of her breath on my face. I'm going to kiss her.

She sits up suddenly, her eyes full of fear.

"It's okay," I assure her, "it's me."

"I had to hide," she says. "I was so afraid."

"You should have gone upstairs."

"I did till I was sure they were gone. But I thought you wouldn't want me to stay up there."

I shake my head. "I don't mind. I did, but. . . . Did you see . . . ?"

"Your work?" She nods. "I like it." Outside the waves crash and the wind howls. Jill shivers and pulls her jacket around her.

"I thought you might be cold in the barn tonight. I took this blanket there, before I figured out you came here."

"I couldn't stay in the barn when the cops came," she says. "I didn't know if you might . . . tell." She thanks me for the blanket, stands up, and goes on to explain. "Once you knew the cops were after me, I didn't know if you'd be sorry you helped me."

"I'm not sorry."

She bites her bottom lip and shakes her head.

"I brought you some more to eat," I say, "and my Walkman. I don't know what you like, but here's some Dylan, David Bowie, and Barenaked Ladies. I figured being a dancer you might like music to keep you company till you have to go." Saying that out loud, I realize how much I hope it won't be soon.

"Chad, why are you being so nice to me?"

Yeah, why am I? I bumble around about how I wasn't painting right and how she gave me something. I hardly understand it myself, so I don't do too hot explaining it to her. But I know if she hadn't come along I wouldn't have got back to my painting.

"Besides," I finish up, "I like you." It's good it's dark. I can feel my face going more shades of red than are in anybody's paint box.

"I like you too, Chad," she says, and I think my insides are going to burst. "But I didn't do anything for you. You did it yourself."

"What I was doing before you came along was a mess. You did something."

"I'm glad," she says, and turns to the window. "Do you always paint up there?"

"Yeah."

"This whole place is so beautiful," she says. "Wouldn't you like to work out on the hills, and on the beach?"

"I used to paint all around here," I tell her, "when my mom was alive. But everyone thinks I quit after she died."

"But Chad, you're so good."

"Only since today," I tell her. "But that has nothing to do with it." I go on to explain how my dad's been crowding me and how I have to keep this apart from him.

"Kind of like this part of you belongs to your mother," she says, "and you don't want to give it to him."

"It's not just my painting," I say. "I don't want to do anything with him. He drives me crazy just being around."

Jill flops down on the fish box by the window. "And here I've been thinking you've got such a great thing with your dad, going for walks together, working on projects, and everything."

"From what you've said about your dad, anybody else's would look good."

She bites her lip and looks away. I hope she's not going to cry again.

"The stuff about the gambling and the money for my dancing — that's really horrid. But you know what I really hate?" Clouds covering the face of the moon darken her face. "It's how he can be so hard on my brother, accusing him of ruining his life and everything, when he's made such a mess of his own."

"What's your brother done?"

"His girlfriend got pregnant and instead of dumping her, he plans to marry her."

"How old is he?"

"Mark's eighteen and Amy almost is. The thing is, he's not planning on quitting school like Dad says he will, and he can keep working at the gas station. And Sobey's will take Amy back after she has the baby. They'll do fine."

"It doesn't sound like Mark's going to do a whole lot better than your dad, if you ask me."

"Well I didn't ask you," she flares. "And just 'cause your family's got gobs of money and can afford to throw out leftovers to some stray, it doesn't give you the right to go passing judgement on my brother." She says *my brother* like he's some kind of hero.

"Hang on," I interrupt. "You're here, all upset 'cause of the mess your family's in, and okay, maybe your brother doesn't have your dad's gambling problem, but do you honestly think he's going to provide any better for his baby pumping gas than your dad's done for you?"

"Material things aren't all that matters," she snaps. "But I wouldn't expect a rich creep like you to understand that."

"Understand what?"

"Mark and Amy don't have to be rich to love their kid."

"I never said they did."

Rocks and waves echo along the shore, over and over, rumbling and crashing. If arguing with Jill didn't feel so awful, I'd think it was funny how the sea seems to be in the same foul temper as her. Except Jill's is wearing down. The sea is still thrashing around out there.

Quieter now, Jill says, "I guess I better get back to the barn, if that's still okay."

"You can stay here if you want." Her dark eyes, lit up again by the unveiling of the moon, tell me how much that means to her.

"I didn't think. . . ."

"You're the one who's mad, not me. Come on," I say, "if you're going to sleep here, we should get your stuff upstairs. I might be the first one here in the morning, but you never know."

I go to take the blanket and the bag. She puts her hand on my arm. "I'm real mixed up about my family," she says. "Thanks for letting me stay here."

It feels awkward and wonderful with her touching me like that, even through the sleeve of my sweatshirt, but all I do is shrug and say, "It's alright."

I'm glad it's darker upstairs. I think if she looked at my paintings in the light, with me there, it would feel like I was standing in front of her naked.

"Maybe you should just tell him," Jill says. "Tell him you've gotta paint, that it helps keep your mother with you somehow. And that you've gotta paint on your own. He'd have to understand, wouldn't he?"

"You haven't done so great working things out with your parents that you should be telling me how to deal with mine, okay?" It's not mean how I say it, I just don't think she's qualified to comment. She's not that easily put off though.

"But what about your grandfather?" she says. "Being a writer, wouldn't he understand?"

"My grandfather's not a writer."

"P.G. Merrill? Isn't that your grandfather?"

"Yeah, but. . . ."

"There's a book of his downstairs," Jill insists. "Didn't you know?"

I shake my head.

"I'll show you."

Even after I dig the flashlight out of my pocket and shine it on the cover where Gramp's written his name, I don't believe it. My heart's thumping and I don't know if it's from trying to figure out what this means or if it's from how close to me Jill is. But it also occurs to me that I've been "looking for my sweatshirt" for a while, and I should be getting back.

"You should probably be getting back to the house, eh, Chad?"

"Will you be okay here?" Dumb question. What choice does she have?

"Let me just come outside with you for a minute. I love to feel the wind when a storm's blowing up."

The wind catches the door when I open it. Jill wrestles it shut. A huge wave crashes near the Fish House. Cool spray mists over us. Shadows are dancing wildly across the face of the moon.

Jill takes hold of my arm with both her hands. "A secret in the old barn," she says. "A secret in the Fish House. You're good at secrets, aren't you."

I nod and lean a little closer so she can hear above the din of the sea. "But sometimes," I say, "it's nice to have somebody to share a secret with."

Along the length of the shoreline the thunderous grumble of battered rocks echoes far into the distance.

"I have a secret too, Chad."

"Do you want to tell me?"

"Then it won't be a secret."

"Oh, yeah." The phosphorescent foam rises and falls on the waves.

"But I think I'll tell you anyway." She leans forward and her warm lips brush against my cheek.

I turn toward them.

"You're right," Jill whispers. She leans closer again.

This time I can taste the sea spray on her lips.

"It is nice . . ."

Oh nice. We kiss again.

". . . to have someone . . ."

Oh, nice, nice. Again.

". . . to share a secret with."

Sunday

Jill

Hard rain pelts the Fish House roof. Gusts of wind buffet against its walls. I'm going home today. At least that's what I wake up thinking. Something last night, something about Chad making me spell it out, what's important in a family, was strange.

It kind of reminded me of this guy Max in a book my dad used to read me. At the end of the story, after Max has been with the wild things for a while, he wants to go back home, to "where he's loved best of all".

My parents might not be doing such a hot job of showing it, but that's kind of how I feel. And they're who I've got.

I guess I'm who they've got too. Not that I've thought lately that it mattered, but seeing the cops pull up outside Chad's yesterday, and go into this houseful of together family people, got me thinking. My parents reported me missing 'cause they want me back.

But so what? Nothing's changed since I left. Except Mark's gone now too and they know I lied about Sheila's. Nothing's going to change if I go back either.

Dad'll never go to one of those group things Chad mentioned and Ma's going to stick by him no matter what.

Maybe it'd be easier to head west. If I could get on the Yarmouth ferry to the States somehow....

I huddle in the corner, wrapping Chad's blanket tightly around me, wishing he were here. I think of how his arms felt around me out on the rocks, the smell of his neck, and the taste of the sea on his lips. I'm sure when I'm with him again, going anywhere's going to be the last thing on my mind.

Oh well. With this storm I won't be seeing him or leaving here for a while. I breathe warm air onto my hands, rub them together under the blanket before getting up.

I stare out the rain-battered window into the wet. The storm is whipping at the trees along the shore, tearing up the sea in choppy peaks. Sitting on the chunk of driftwood, I've still got Chad's blanket wrapped around me. It's cold, but also — never mind, it sounds stupid.

Chad

I wipe condensation off the kitchen window, stare out into the driving rain. Gramp pokes at the fire in the woodstove.

I stayed with Jill at the Fish House last night for as long as I dared. I can still taste her softness this morning.

"A storm system moving into the area," a voice on the radio says, "caused temperatures along the coast to dip during the night. High winds and rain are expected to be with us through much of the day. It is five minutes after ten."

The rain beats down. The branches of the trees whip around as if trying to escape the lashing winds. The heat from the woodstove has taken the chill out of the kitchen, but the blanket I took Jill last night won't be much help to her. The window rattles in its frame. She'll be warmer than if she was in the Old Barn, but not a lot.

I want to be with her again.

"Chad, I'm talking to you."

"Sorry, Gran. What did you say?"

"I've asked you three times," Gran says from under the folds of material she's pinning together, "to put the kettle on for some tea. You're getting as deaf as your grandfather."

"I was just thinking about the storm," I say, filling the kettle at the sink.

"I don't remember ever lighting a fire in the stove in July," says Gramp, "not even the year we had snow in June." He throws in another log.

"This is a strange one all right," agrees Gran.

I take a deep breath. "I think I'll go down to the Fish House and watch the storm up close for a while."

"Oh, Chad," fusses Gran, "it's too cold. You'll get wet."

"I'll wear a jacket under my raincoat," I say, getting my things from the hook. "I'll be okay."

"And I'll come with you," says Dad.

"No, Gordon," says Gramp, "you stay here and read your book. I'll go with Chad."

They're arguing over who's going to come with me and inside I'm screaming. What good will going to the Fish House do me, or Jill, if either one of them comes along? Finally I blurt out, "Can't I just go by myself?"

What I see in Dad's eyes makes me feel like a heel, but he's decided not to come, and right now that matters more. But Gramp, surprisingly, doesn't let go. "This is a marvellous storm," he says. "At my age this might be my last chance to enjoy a good one. The waves will be crashing up the face of the Fish House, I'll bet you." He goes into the mudroom and comes back with his rubber boots and raincoat. "Come on, Chad, let's go."

Well, what can you say when an old guy pulls out the "this might be my last chance" number. He's been saying that for years, but after last winter's heart attack, I don't feel like I can joke about it.

"Let's take along a thermos of tea," he says. "It'll be a mite chilly down there."

A splash of cold rain blows in as we head out. The wind bangs the door shut behind us.

The rain pelts our olive green raincoats, drips from our hoods. Our boots *squoosh* in the sodden grass. Gramp turns his face up to the sky as though it would receive warm sunshine instead of cold rain. "Fine day for a stroll in the woods, eh, Chad?" He laughs. His face and his raincoat are shiny wet. He looks like a green monster that has crawled out of the creepy depths of somewhere.

"Yes, sir," I try to play along.

"Whuh?"

"I said, Yes sir. Fine day, sir."

It's calmer in the woods. The trees drip, their colour rich with the rain. It's weird that I feel so overwhelmed with green here. If I were painting this, I'd be using mostly Payne's Grey.

I should run ahead so I can tell Jill how my plan went wrong, with everyone awake early because of the storm, and then Gramp insisting on coming too. But Gramp's friendly hand on my shoulder squelches that idea.

Down by the shore the wind rips into us full force again. We clutch our flapping hoods. Our coats snap at our legs. I pull open the heavy wooden door of the Fish House, swollen with the damp, and holler, "We made it, Gramp," to let Jill know fast that I'm not alone.

Inside the Fish House the grumbling sea and yowling storm are only slightly muffled by the thick walls. We take off our dripping raincoats and hang them on nails near the door. Gramp sets down the thermos on the fish box and we stand by the window, watching the storm bashing the shore, and once in a while, as Gramp predicted, the Fish House itself. We stand there for several minutes, neither of us saying anything.

"Something on your mind, son?" Gramp says finally.

"No," I answer quickly, "not really."

"Do you suppose that's a boat out there?" Gramp asks. "See? Out that way a bit?"

"I don't see anything, Gramp."

"My eyes just playing tricks, I guess."

"Must be. Nobody'd be out there today."

Several more minutes pass, and I can feel how still Jill is sitting, not ten feet away. For something to do, because I'm going crazy just standing here, I unscrew the top of the thermos and pour some tea into it.

"I didn't bring the tea for you, Chad."

Surprised, I apologize and hand the steaming cup to Gramp.

"It's not for me either." Gramp pours the tea back into the thermos.

"Then who'd you bring it for?" An especially high wave pounds against the rocks and up the side of the Fish House. "Gramp?" I have to look away from his probing eyes.

"I thought your friend in the Old Barn might appreciate a hot cup of tea on a morning like this."

The racket of the storm is almost louder than his voice, but Gramp's words send a powerful shock through me. I fix my gaze on the water pooling under the dripping raincoats. "I didn't think anyone knew," I finally manage to say.

"So, it wasn't just my eyes playing tricks again, eh?"

I shake my head. Should I tell him she's not in the barn any more, she's upstairs?

"I didn't think so."

"How did you know, Gramp?"

"Let's just say a little bird told me."

"Has your little bird spoken to anyone else around here?"

"I'm the only birdwatcher in this family," Gramp says, "so I doubt it."

"Did you know she was there when the police came yesterday?" I ask him. "Why haven't you made her leave?"

"Sometimes people have to run away, get a bit of distance between themselves and their problem, before they can turn around and face it," he says.

"So, you were really thinking of her when you suggested bringing the tea?"

"I've been trying to figure out what to do about her ever since I woke up this morning and the house was so darn cold. I figured she couldn't stay holed up in the Old Barn for long in this weather, she'd be catching pneumonia."

"Why didn't you just tell me you knew?"

"I knew she was supposed to be a secret," he says, taking his raincoat from its hook. "And you're not the only one around here who can keep a secret, you know."

I try not to look at the fish box. I'm still not sure whether to tell him Jill's here, or let him go to the barn and think she's left.

There's a scraping sound above and the ladder appears through the hole in the ceiling. I wish I had a camera to catch the look on Gramp's face. Wrapped in our blanket Jill backs down the ladder. I introduce them to each other.

"Good God," Gramp says, shaking Jill's hand, "I thought my time had come and you were the angel of mercy come to deliver me." He laughs at himself, then says, "Would you like some tea?"

Jill

I should probably feel more nervous of this guy who owns the Trespassers Will Be Prosecuted sign, but I don't. I like him immediately. Maybe it's because of the way he reacts to my appearance, or else because he's a bit like Chad, the way he stands or the expression around his mouth or something. Or maybe I just can't help but like someone who calls his diary "Rocks and Dune Grass". But I am a little in awe of him. When he offers me tea, I stammer, "Yes please." My hands are trembling when I take the steaming cup. "Thank you."

"You're lucky that ladder didn't collapse on you," Chad's grandfather says. "The things so rotten, it hasn't been used in years. The floor up there too, for that matter."

I almost say, "But Chad...", but stop myself in time. I shiver then, and gulp down the hot sweet tea. I never put sugar in my tea, but this morning it tastes good.

"This is a devil of a place to get acquainted," Chad's grandfather says. "What say we head up to the house? There's a nice fire going in the kitchen."

"But what about Gran and Dad?" Chad asks.

"It'll be fine," his grandfather insists.

"Jill doesn't have a raincoat," Chad says. "She'll get soaked."

"The rain's letting up," the old man says. "I'll take yours and drape it over me. My big one will cover the pair of you. Don't argue now. We've got to get your friend here someplace warm."

Chad's grandfather shoves open the door. The rain's dwindled to a light drizzle. "Just leave the blanket," he says, stepping out into the wind. "We can get that later."

In the doorway Chad drapes the other raincoat around the two of us, so we're each holding one side.

His grandfather's already heading into the woods. Before we follow him Chad touches a hand to the side of my face and kisses me. "Remember that," he whispers, "whatever happens, okay?"

I step back into the protection of the Fish House and let go of my side of the raincoat, so I can wrap both my arms around Chad's waist and be close to him again. I kiss the little hollow under his Adam's apple. I'd tell him now, before all his family's around, that I'm leaving today, but with his arms around me again, it's not what I feel like saying. At this moment I'm so happy the only thing that could make me happier is if me and Chad hugging each other could go on forever.

But his grandfather expects we're behind him, so we arrange the raincoat over us again and go out.

The wind's at our backs crossing the rocks, and among the trees it's quiet. Crossing the open field I blurt it out, "I'm going home today." Chad's grandfather's almost at the house. "Why don't I just go now."

Chad's face looks stricken. He lets go of his part of the raincoat and pulls it closed around me. "Stay till it stops raining. Please."

"It's almost stopped now," I tell him. "And I don't want to go in there." I reach up and brush the wet hair out of his eyes. "I won't forget you."

As if Chad has some connection with the powers that control the weather, the sky opens up right then, pouring down hard angry slashes of rain. We run to the steps and, feeling Chad's hand at my back, I follow his grandfather into the house.

The kitchen's warm, its windows steamy. Chad's father looks up from a book. His grandmother looks up from her sewing. It feels like a room full of people, staring. I can feel my damp and dirty clothes clinging to me, my stringy hair hanging in frizzy tangles. I look down at my soggy sneakers, wishing the floor would open underneath me.

"Close the door please, Chad," his grandmother says. "You're letting in the cold."

Chad

"Well, well," Dad says, "what have we here?"

Gramp says, "Take the girl upstairs, Edna. She needs a hot bath and some clean clothes."

"Isn't this the girl," Dad says, "that the police were here about yesterday?"

"That's right," says Gramp, "and she's chilled. Edna, please get Jill what she needs for a bath. And something to put on while her clothes are in the dryer."

Gran's lips are pursed tight as she leads Jill out of the kitchen. I guess her helpful nature's been pushed past its limit.

"Did you know she was on our property when the police were here, Chad?" asks Dad. "You should have said something."

"I believe," says Gramp, "that loyalty to one's friends is a worthy priority."

"Friend?" Dad exclaims. "She's not that, Chad — surely."

Gran comes back with Jill's damp clothes. "I remember where I saw her," she says. "She was walking down our road when we were going into town yesterday." She takes her damp bundle into the laundry room behind the pantry.

"What's she doing here?" Dad asks.

"It doesn't matter," I say. "She's going home when the storm lets up."

"We'd better call the police," says Gran, "and let them know she's here."

"Do we have to?" I say. "She's going home anyway."

"The police can just make sure," says Gran, reaching for the phone.

"Let's wait and talk to Jill first," interrupts Gramp. "In the meantime, why doesn't someone find out what time the bus to Halifax goes? You call, Gordon, while Chad changes into some dry clothes."

None of this discussion feels like it has anything to do with the girl I spent yesterday afternoon on the beach with, or that time last night at the Fish House. I go to my room and change. I stay there, listening to the sounds of Jill in the bath, looking out the window to where she bathed yesterday with the sun glinting off her and the water, thinking about that and the paintings it led to.

Today's a day for a dramatic seascape, using different shades of grey to capture the different textures of the clouds and rocks, the cold choppiness of the sea. I stay in my room until the bathroom door opens.

"I've really gotta go," says Jill when I meet her in the hall. "Can you go see if my clothes are dry?" She pulls on the baggy sides of Gran's lavender sweatpants. "I can't wear this."

I go down to get her clothes out of the dryer and find out that the bus stops at the Irving at ten past three, that Gramp will pay for her ticket, and Gran will drive her out to meet it.

I take Jill her clothes and tell her the plan.

"I'm not staying till then," she says. "I don't belong here. I'll just walk out to the highway."

"It's pretty far."

"I've done it before," she reminds me.

"I'll come with you."

I wait in the hall for Jill to change into her own clothes and we go downstairs. I tell Dad and Gran and Gramp that I'm going to walk Jill out to the highway to catch her bus.

"Thank you for offering to take me," says Jill, "but I don't want to be any more trouble."

Gran mutters that it would be no trouble, but she's clearly relieved to have Jill leaving. I imagine Gramp was saying he'd take her and Gran only insisted on doing it to keep him from driving. She fusses about him a lot. She always has, but more since last winter.

The charcoal sky has a big blue crack in it, but I grab a couple of raincoats off the hooks just in case, and something for us to eat out of the pantry. We say goodbye. Gramp wishes Jill luck.

Passing by the Old Barn I get an idea. "Come back to the Fish House with me?" I say. "There's time. Please."

Jill

I'm glad Chad's walking to the bus with me. I would have hated having his father or grandmother drive me. Not that they'd have been nasty or anything, but I could tell they weren't like Gramp. If they'd known where I was when the cops came round, things would've turned out a lot different.

Well, maybe not a lot different, 'cause it turns out I'm going home anyway. But I'm glad I got to figure out for myself that I want to, instead of somebody making me. Also, if Chad's dad and grandmother knew I was here they wouldn't have waited for any cops to show up asking about me. I'd have been out of here. Then I would never have fallen for Chad. As in head over heels. Corny eh?

I think it's so cool that he's a painter. With a grandfather who's a writer. What a family.

But it's weird how Chad didn't know about his grandfather's writing. Not that a diary's supposed to be public, but he had no idea. So there's Chad painting away in secret upstairs, and his grandfather writing away in secret downstairs – maybe all families are a little weird.

I bet that old guy's diary would make interesting reading.

Going back to the Fish House might not be such a hot idea. What if I chicken out about facing my parents once I'm down there again? But Chad seems so intent. And it'll be a cozier place for goodbye than the bus stop outside the Irving.

The warm humid woods are like a blanket wrapped around us. It's like we've thrown it off when we step into the fresh breeze.

A shaft of sunlight breaks through a crack in the clouds, splashing the rocks with colour. There's another shift in the clouds, and the sea loses its leaden greyness and shimmers.

The ladder's still leaning into the hole from this morning. Chad starts up. I'm going to follow him, but he says, "Stay there, okay? I want it to be just the way you were the first time I saw you." He disappears into the upper room.

"What?" I ask. "What are you doing?"

He sits cross-legged beside the hole with his sketchpad and pencil.

"Chad, no, I feel silly." I step away from the ladder.

"You don't look silly," he says. "Please?"

I move slowly back and look up at him. This isn't what I thought he had in mind when he suggested coming down here.

"That's perfect," Chad says. "Except that hand. No, leave that one in your pocket. The other one, put it on the ladder. Yeah, like that. That's the way it was."

"You don't remember that," I argue.

"I do," he insists. "Chin up just a little."

I try not to smile, but do as he asks, glad that's how he thinks of me, with my chin up.

Chad's pencil flicks around his paper and in just a few minutes he asks me to come up. He pulls the chunk of driftwood away from the window a bit. The opening in the clouds is growing larger and the mixture of sun and cloud is doing incredible things to the surface of the sea. Chad asks me to sit down.

He unscrews the lid from a jar of water and opens up a box of paints. He looks at the sketch in his lap, then at me. He squeezes a fresh blob of creamy paint onto the smooth inner surface of a large shell. It feels like a gentle squeeze on my heart. I sit there while he paints, breathing in the sea smells trapped in the wood of the Fish House, listening to the slap-lopping of the sea outside, watching him get lost in his painting. It makes me want to jump up and dance.

Till I remember I'm on my way home, and I feel afraid.

Such a strange mix of emotions tumble around inside me that I can't tell if it's a long time or a short time later when Chad holds up his work and says it's finished. It's me, of course, in the Fish House. My eyes are like a reflection of the sea, the colours he's used, and the moodiness he's captured too.

A tiny pool near one of the eyes in the painting spills over. "Oh, you've ruined it," I tell him.

"I don't think so," Chad says gently. He reaches over and with his finger strokes a tear from my cheek. He kisses me then and I know I'd better go.

My heart's aching as I look around the Fish House, wanting to take it all in — Chad, the sea that's so much a part of it, the paintings on the wall I discovered last night. I want to take all of it with me.

Chad goes to where his paintings are hanging and tacks up the wet one he's just finished. He takes down the picture of the old barn, silvery grey against soft watercolour hills, and the abstract one that's me dancing in the sea. He rolls them up together. "I'd like you to keep these . . ." He holds the roll out to me and shrugs. ". . . if you'd like to have them."

"Both of them?" I say.

"It's okay," he says, "there'll be lots more."

When I reach for them my hand touches Chad's on the roll. "I'd like to."

Chad brushes a finger over my hand. We both know it's not just his pictures I'd like.

"I better get going," I say. "The bus...."

Chad tears a corner off a piece of paper and writes down his address. "Will you write and tell me what happens when you get home?"

"Okay." I slip his address into my jeans pocket. I write down my address for him too. "If you write me and tell me about the rest of your summer."

Out of habit I guess Chad puts the ladder back by the wall under the maps. I ask him to show me where on the map we are exactly and he shows me. Then he kisses me again and we hold each other for a minute. But I've gotta go. And I'm ready.

We step outside. The wind's blowing up strong again and there's no trace of blue in the ominous clouds.

"It looks like this storm might not be finished yet," Chad says. "But we can probably make it to the bus before it starts."

This is where I have to say goodbye to Chad, here at the Fish House. I know it, suddenly.

"Don't come with me to the bus, Chad," I say.

"But...."

I shake my head. "I have to do this alone." And before I can change my mind, I go.

Chad

I guess if anybody should understand her needing to be alone, it's me. I watch her go, hoping she'll change her mind and ask me to come, or at least turn around and wave. But she doesn't.

She's gone. Like a sandcastle washed away by the tide. Boy, can she make me think dumb things. Besides being cornball, it's not even true. Because when the tide's done with a sandcastle there's no trace of its ever having been there. But there's part of Jill in me that will never go away.

Another dumb thought. Only, not really. Jill wasn't here for long, but she's done something to me. I want to be alone for a while too, so I head along the rocks at the base of the cliff. For one thing I feel about five years older than I did two days ago, even since I came this way yesterday afternoon. But something doesn't fit.

Some of the rocks are slippery from the wet, so I try to stick to the rough and wrinkled-looking ones. All along the shore the ocean mumbles and smashes and spits. It churns and gurgles and rocks. It takes me a long time to get as far as Whaleback. When I climb up the rock, the mist is thicker again, almost thick enough to call rain.

But it hasn't yet hidden the Fish House, where so much has happened in the past twenty-four hours. Not just with Jill, with my painting too.

That's what doesn't fit. The kid hiding in the Fish House with his box of paints — that's not me any more.

The surf crashes against the rock, sending heavy spray up its hard face.

Going to the Fish House to paint was my big statement of independence — I'm going to paint and I'm going to do it myself. But hiding out like that's just childish, isn't it?

Sure it means Dad isn't going to horn in on what I'm doing. But keeping it a secret doesn't make me free of him. It just means I can't paint wherever or whenever I feel like it, and that ties me just as much as if I let him come and paint beside me. Doesn't it?

I slide down Whaleback to the wet sand. I jam my fists in my pockets, stride along the beach. Powerful waves rumble toward me, wash in hissing silvery sheets up the sand, then retreat. Over and over, up and down the length of the beach.

I'm going to have to tell him.

I take a deep breath of the salty air, try to make myself slow down, and let the rhythm of the sea calm me. But it doesn't.

Sandpipers tiptoe frantically at the waters' edge. Mist hangs in the air, some of it falling now as rain. It's not like yesterday, when it rolled in from nowhere. But something about it — as I get closer to the rocks between the small beach and the big one an incredible uneasiness washes through me. It's going to happen again. I can feel it in the way it's moving, rolling into shapes . . .

I turn back toward Whaleback and start to run. But it's as if the figure of my mother has appeared again and I can't move fast enough in the sand to escape her. *What do you want?* I want to yell. *You told me to paint. I've painted. Why can't you leave me alone?* My face is soaked and I know it's not just the rain.

I charge headlong into something solid and let out an agonized groan.

"Chad, Chad, what is it?"

It's Dad.

"Why did she have to go? It hurts," I wail. "And it's my fault."

"It's not your fault," Dad assures me. "She simply doesn't belong here."

He thinks I'm talking about Jill. "I mean Mom. Why don't you hate me? You'd still have her if. . . ."

Dad grabs me to his chest with his arms. "No, no, you mustn't think. . . ."

"But Dad, it's true. If I had taken the bus instead . . ." There's no need to finish. He knows.

You'd think he'd try and convince me it wasn't my fault, and it could happen to anybody any time, wouldn't you? But what Dad tells me just about knocks my socks off. He squeezes my shoulders and says that after Mom died, he wished I was in the car too when the truck hit it.

I figure right about now's when I'm supposed to run into the ocean and never stop. But I don't. I stop crying. Maybe this is what I've been needing to hear.

He loosens his grip on my shoulders. "I wished you would just go away and leave me alone."

"But you were always around, wanting to do stuff."

"Do you think I was proud of the way I felt?" He lets go of me then and we start walking toward Whaleback. "Everything I lived for ended when your mother died," he says. "I know that's an awful thing for me to say to you, Chad. But you were her son in so many ways, not mine." He struggles with his words, but I think he's trying to say that he always felt kind of on the outside, and he thought when she died I'd need him more, but it didn't seem like I did, and somehow with feeling guilty about not really wanting much to do with me, that's made him try that much more to be part of my life.

It's all so mixed up. I never thought parents could be so confused. I end up wondering if I should go live with Gran and Gramp in Ottawa or something.

He asks me if I want to and I say no. But, is that what *he* wants? "Not unless you want me to," I say quickly. "I could . . ."

"No," he cuts me off. "I don't want you to. You're my son. I want to try and be a father to you."

Oh, no, here we go again. "Isn't that what you've been doing?"

"I think maybe I've been trying to be your father and your mother, with a lot of unresolved feelings mixed in with that. But your mother's gone."

It's the first time he's said that, maybe even to himself.

"We're getting wet," he says. "Let's go back to the house."

"What were you doing out here?" I ask him. "You could tell the storm was coming back, couldn't you?"

"It didn't matter," he says. "Sometimes I just need to be alone."

Don't I know it.

"Do you think — would you mind — coming to the Fish House first?" I seem to be asking a lot of people there lately. But this time is different. No kidding.

Jill

The smells of Chad and moss and pine and mushrooms — I think I'll always lump those things together. They're what I take with me as I leave the Merrills' woods.

The trio of mailboxes, where I first discovered coming down this road was a mistake, nod me a polite farewell. Except it's hard to believe it was a mistake, in the end.

How would things have turned out if I'd found Sheila's place that afternoon? I'd have stepped right into her parents' breakup, and wouldn't have been ready to go home when they all headed back to Halifax. Would I have gone anyway? Or made a break for the Yarmouth ferry? I might have been hitching my way west by now.

I could still do that.

There's something different about the decrepit house with its rusted car and pot of weeds out front. Is it just that the rain's made it look fresher, more alive, hopeful? I look back. No. It's the tricycle beside the car, a brand new red trike. Left out in the rain, it won't take long for it to match the rest of the ruins. Just as I'm thinking this, the front door opens and a little mop of a kid toddles out and drags the trike into the empty wood shelter at the side of the house.

The wind pushes me on, as if I can't be trusted to continue along the road fast enough to catch the bus without its help. Not that I'm seriously tempted to go it on my own out in B.C. But knowing the mess I'm going home to doesn't exactly make we want to dance.

Well, it does actually. That's the great thing about dancing. When you're happy, it expresses that. And when you're not, it takes you somewhere else. I'll miss that. Unless I can figure some way to pay for my classes.

I'm not far from the highway when a car crunches on the gravel road behind me. I almost stick out my thumb, figure I'll go whichever way it's going. If they're going toward Yarmouth, then I'm not meant to go home, and if they're going toward Halifax, well, fine, I'll have saved myself bus fare. A muddy yellow car slishes by in the seconds I stall getting my thumb out there.

When I get to the Irving the car's there filling up. The guy behind the wheel's asking the kid at the pump whether there'll be a line-up for the Yarmouth ferry. A second chance.

I hoist my knapsack higher on my shoulder and shift Chad's paintings. It's chilly in the damp wind, but I'm sweating inside my jacket. Home – my con man father, my self-sacrificing gutless mother, no Mark, the grilling I'm sure to face and the tighter-than-ever watch over everything I do –

I can't do it.

I step toward the yellow car, shoving my hands in my jacket pockets. The two bills Chad's grandfather slipped me are wadded up in one of them, and I hesitate. It's the bus fare the old guy gave me, because he trusted me to get on the bus and go home, where I belong.

Chad

Battered by the wind and wet, Dad and I start across the rocks. We're getting close to the Fish House when Dad says something all mathematical about tide schedules and lunar eclipses. I know a day or two ago it would have really bugged me, because Mom would never look at the sea or the tides or the moon and think about it like that. But now I realize it hasn't been how Dad thinks and how he lives exactly that's been churning me up. It's that he's alive, and Mom isn't. It's not how he eats his egg, it's that he can and she can't.

I don't know why it should matter to know that, but it does, and I can listen to Dad without wishing he weren't there.

I'm not expecting anyone to be in the Fish House. But Jill's changed her mind. For that first split second after we open the door, that's what I think.

It's Gramp sitting on the fish box by the window. He's writing with a fine felt marker in that notebook. The look on his face when he turns toward the open door is like a kid who's been caught with his hand in the cookie jar. "Gramp," I exclaim, mostly because I'm still surprised to see him, "what are you doing here?"

He pulls himself together. "I told you you're not the only one around here who can have secrets."

"Father," says Dad, "what are you doing? Should you be out again in this weather? What were you writing?"

"Just a few rambling ideas."

Dad nods toward the thick notebook. "It looks like you've been at it for some time," he says. "I didn't know."

"That's hardly surprising," Gramp says.

Dad shifts on his feet and it all feels a bit awkward. Maybe this isn't the time to bring up about my painting.

Gramp says, less harshly, "We haven't been close, Gordon. But I thought it was time for me to get down some things that might not get said otherwise. What are you doing here, Chad? I thought you were escorting your friend to the bus."

"She decided to go by herself," I say and blurt out before I lose my nerve, "and I wanted to show Dad something." I put the ladder into the space in the ceiling and start up.

"Chad, no," Dad says, "the ladder's broken, the floor's punky."

"It's okay," I tell him. "I'm careful. You wait here."

I leave the jar of murky water and the shell-palette and bring the oak box and the paintings off the wall — the thistle, the pine tree, and the one of Mom's ghost, or whatever that was. The one of Jill isn't dry, so I leave it.

It belongs here anyway, somehow.

Jill

As the bus signals the exit for Halifax, my stomach does a major flip. I'm almost home. Will anyone be there? Did Gramp or anybody call and tell the police I'd been "found"?

Will Chad really write to me? *I said I would,* he said that first morning when I doubted he was coming to the barn. I unroll the pictures he gave me. The grey barn's almost silver, and I'm reminded of the magical scene out its window that morning. The other one makes me feel all tingly, when I think of Chad painting me that way. It's good Ma won't be able to tell what it is.

I roll the pictures back up carefully, trying to imagine them on the wall in my tiny room. I wish Mark could see them.

I take the sand dollar out of my chest pocket where I've put it for safe-keeping. Holding it between my palms I close my eyes and imagine the five little chips of shell inside breaking away, emerging from the little hole in the bottom, and taking wing. When I get home the peace doves are there, on the windowsill of our apartment. With Mark waiting inside.

Why can't he be there?

Too hard. It's easier to think about Chad, even though it really did hurt to leave him. I couldn't let myself think of him after I left his woods or I'd have been turning back so I could feel just one more time the length of his body pressed against me, his arms wrapped around me, my cheek against his. God, I can't think about this either.

I guess I always figured leaving somebody you love was hard, and that Ma stayed with Dad 'cause she was too weak, too scared not to. But she must've been one tough cookie to stick around with the kind of problems they've got. It would've been easier for her to dump him when everything started going wrong. But that's not what she did.

I'm not saying I think she did right staying with Dad. And I don't know if I'm doing the right thing either. But going home, for now, and giving things there another chance – it's what I've got to do.

Chad

Dad's face goes hard when he sees Mom's old paint box and he looks a little pale. But there's no turning back. I spread the paintings out on the floor and brace myself for whatever's coming.

"So you are a painter, after all," says Gramp.

"I know it's hard to make a good living," I say, "but . . ."

"Never mind that," Gramp interrupts. "You have something more important than security. Something I never had." He gets up slowly from the fish box, unfolding each bend in his body one at a time.

Dad turns away from my pictures, looks instead at the navigational charts on the back wall.

"What do you mean, Gramp?"

"When I was a young man," he says and I can tell this is going to be a long one, "I dreamed of being a writer. But I never wrote anything. I went into law because it was safer. And I was a good lawyer too. So I stayed with it, because I had a wife and son to support. But all the years I spent going in to my office I still dreamed. Well, my son grew up and then I retired and I thought, Now I can write my book. But I got scared all over again. Someone might call it the work of an old fool. So I didn't write it. Then last winter I had that heart attack. Scared the bejeepers out of me that did. My time for making excuses had just about run out. So I got started. It wasn't so hard – I figured I'd probably die before I got near finishing it. But I'm still here. And it's almost done."

"Extraordinary," Dad says.

"Not so extraordinary," Gramp says. "Just the ramblings of a foolish old man. I'm going back to the house now before that rain starts up again."

He leaves, but doesn't take the notebook with him. He doesn't put it back in the box where it was when Jill discovered it last night either.

"Well," says Dad.

There doesn't seem to be anything else to say. I feel a bit upstaged by Gramp's story. It makes the whole secret around my painting seem absurd. Till Dad says, "I was glad you weren't painting any more after your mom died. I thought it would be too painful a reminder of her somehow."

I wish I'd left the one of Mom upstairs. Suddenly thrumming sheets of rain are beating against the Fish House. Maybe I should have left the whole lot up there.

"But we aren't going to forget her either way, are we?" he says, "so I suppose you'd better do what you have to do."

It's not quite the reaction I might have hoped for. But it's probably not the end of it either.

I don't know how anything I started this summer is going to end.

Will I be a painter "when I grow up"? I don't know. But Dad and I have started redoing the floor of the Fish House with that wood in the Old Barn so I can use it for a studio.

Will I hear from Jill again? I don't know that either. But I wrote her a letter last night while Gran was reading *Rocks and Dune Grass: Diary of an Old Man*.

Will I ever forget this summer at Dutchman's Bay? *That's* a dumb question.